# Saved for a Season

Cover Art by Charles Bwembya and Kena Bwembya
Edited by Anita Bunkley

**ISBN:**   978-0-9790414-0-2
0-9790414-0-6

Keeping With the Industry Publishing (KWI)

# Saved for a Season

**A Novel Written by
Kena C. Bwembya**

Saved for a Season

# Chapter One
## The Mistake

"We should just be friends."

Jeff choked on his words as he reached for the glass of water that was recently placed in front of him. Jeff didn't stop for the waitress to leave before springing the news on Tanya. The illicit couple had frequented the restaurant many times during their two-year relationship...if it could properly be called a relationship.

Halo's Bend was a cozy place, situated many miles outside of the city limits. The space allowed for intimate conversations, and Jeff decided long ago that he wanted to keep his relationship with Tanya undercover to protect their fragile bond. They felt safe at Halo's Bend, where they knew very few of the local people and more importantly, very few of the locals knew them.

Embarrassed by Jeff's sudden revelation, Tanya turned her hazel eyes away from the waitress and down to her lap. She fiddled with the cheap napkin placed there in anticipation of her meal, ripping the edges of the flimsy paper, allowing the tattered pieces to float to the floor. She was afraid to look up.

Upon hearing Jeff's words, the waitress lingered a bit longer, obviously in order to hear more of the couple's private conversation, but soon realized no more would be said in her presence. Tanya waited until the waitress walked away, then glanced around to make sure the woman was completely gone before she raised her head again.

Jeff's eyes floated over Tanya as he recognized every piece of jewelry that adorned her body, for he had purchased them all. He watched as she twisted the citrine bracelet, allowing the white gold clasps to open and close rapidly. He wanted her to say something, say anything, but he knew she would wait to speak, choosing her words carefully.

"T," ...that's what Jeff called her when he was treading on thin ice. His voice cleared and was now at a soft whisper. "Are you ok?"

Tanya's eyes glittered with tears as she pursed her naked lips to begin to speak, but nothing came out. She wore no make-up, preferring her red-bone hued skin to remain uncontaminated by foreign substances.

"Tanya you're a great girl..."

"Don't..." Tanya hissed, with a slight raise of her tongue, feeling knots in her stomach begin to start cramping. "Don't patronize me."

"I'm not trying to patronize you." Jeff looked around nervously. "Don't raise your voice."

He turned slowly to see if anyone was listening. His deep brown eyes moved hurriedly from person to person, then rested back on Tanya. She watched as he clenched his jaw, causing deep coco creases to appear and harden his youthful face.

"What are you scared of?" Tanya threw the words at him. "That someone will hear and everyone will know that you're a jerk?"

"This is why we won't work," he threw back.

Tanya flinched. Jeff's tone was cold and unsettling. He had become someone she didn't know. He was nothing like the man she had fallen in love with.

"You're over-the-top, Tanya. You turn everything into a drama."

She rolled her eyes at the dreaded word, drama. Once uttered, it was sure to be the kiss of death for any legitimate relationship, not to mention one that was on the down low.

"But... we've been together for two years."

"What do you expect from me, a ring or something?" he

asked.

Tanya tightly pressed her lips together as she tried to compose herself. She noticed the customers nearest to them had begun to look in their direction and a couple of older women whispered at a table across the room, their voices at a low murmur. However, Tanya could still hear their words.

"She should have known better," the woman in a blue net sweater commented to her friend.

"Ugh. You can't tell these young thangs nothin' and these men are all the same," the friend replied with assuredness.

The attention stirred Tanya's survival instinct. She would not be made to look like a fool. She blocked out her nosy neighbors and stared back at Jeff.

"I expected some respect. I may not be your darling Tristan but I have feelings."

"Respect," Jeff said as he leaned back and cocked his head. "There is nothing respectable about you. This whole thing was a mistake."

His words shot like arrows straight through Tanya and for a brief moment she envisioned herself falling over onto the restaurant's darkened tile floor, gasping for breath.

Jeff clenched his jaw but this time in regret. He didn't want the relationship to end this way, but the words were flying out before he could even own them. But, he knew he had to stand firm. His thoughts drifted to Tristan -- he couldn't lose her, and that was final. He had to make it clear to Tanya that this *friendship* or whatever she wanted to call it was over, even if it meant breaking her down piece by piece.

Tanya watched Jeff as he seemed to lose his concentration, and wondered what he was thinking. Maybe she could change his mind. She could try but what good would it do? She had always known their affair couldn't last forever, and that sooner or later he would have to make a choice. Tanya always believed that in the end she would be the winner of this love war. Yet, the more she pushed, the more withdrawn Jeff became. She should have known the writing was on the wall when Tristan had become more attentive to Jeff. --as if the woman knew she had to fight for him. Then she announced her pregnancy and Tanya knew it was only a matter of time before Jeff would call it quits. No matter how much of a two-timer Jeff was, he had always wanted children and so, there were some lines even he wouldn't cross.

Jeff had stopped caring for Tanya the moment Tristan became pregnant, at least it seemed that way. Tanya had desperately tried to ignore the signs; knowing all along that she was just another notch on his ever extending belt.

"We've been dating..." she started to clamor, losing her backbone.

"Dating? You call this dating?" Jeff snapped. "We were sleeping together. That's it."

"Excuse me?"

Tanya closed her eyes, hoping that when she re-opened them she would be at home in her bed, awakening from a nightmare. But this was no dream and she had put herself in the middle of a fight she was never supposed to win. Jeff had never been hers and all the wishing and hoping to make it so, was not going to change the situation. Desperation flooded Tanya's senses. She had to make him understand what he meant to her, what she meant to him. He had to stay and he *had* to choose her.

"I'm marrying Tristan in three months." He cut into her thoughts. "I love her and I always have."

"She doesn't love you. I do. We belong together," Tanya cried.

"Stop it." Jeff hissed. "You're acting crazy."

"Crazy? I'm crazy? I wasn't crazy when you were all over me last week. What happened between then and now? All of a sudden you've gained a moral backbone? And why did you cheat on Tristan with me? Why tell me you were going to leave her?"

"You wanted a reason to go after me and I gave you one. You didn't need much persuading."

"You're a cheater and liar," Tanya accused. "You think she'll still marry you once she knows you were sleeping with me?"

"Don't act all high and mighty, Tanya. It takes two."

"You came on to *me*, Jeff."

"And you didn't run away."

"You don't even want to marry Tristan. You feel obligated because she's pregnant."

"You don't know me as well as you think you do."

"Oh, okay, so I'm delusional..." Tanya huffed. "You know she's not a stupid woman. She'll find out who and what you are eventually and I will be there to see your perfect little world come crashing down on top of you."

Jeff leaned in, focused on Tanya's eyes. His stare was icy and it made her sense of danger rise. She knew she had gone too far and was suddenly glad to be in a public place.

"If you utter one word to Tristan," he began, his jaw tight, "then I will make sure that Eugene will surely find out who and what you are."

"Oh, please. I'm not dating Eugene."

Tanya laughed off his threat but the laugh was forced. She knew it was a threat she couldn't afford. Eugene was the one friend she had in this world and she could not lose him.

"You act unfazed, but you and I both know he is your *only* friend. But he is also Tristan's only brother." Jeff read her mind and took advantage of her insecurity and leaned in close. "Who do you think he'll choose?"

Tanya's face became hot and caused her already reddened skin to become bright as the tears she had tried to control made her eyes glitter. She tried blinking to keep them from falling but the warm drops fell and wrapped around her chin.

"He's all I have... please don't tell him," she begged.

"I don't care who you hang around but don't you dare say a word to Tristan."

Jeff stood, dropped a twenty dollar bill on the table, and then turned and left. Tanya glanced at the dirty crumpled bill, stained from use, until her vision became so blurred that she could no longer see it clearly. He had tossed the bill away just as easily as he had tossed her out of his life. It stunned her to know that one ill fated encounter had turned into two, and then the lies and secret meetings turned her into the one person she never wanted to be. She had fallen in love with the wrong man. She had fallen in lust and she knew it was deceitful but she craved the attention and pleasure that the affair created. And besides, Jeff had been so easily obliging. It had been a world they created between them, and she had convinced herself that if she tried hard enough, she could gain his trust and devotion and he would leave Tristan for her. That was her fairy tale but Tanya knew that fairy tales were for the story books; at least for her.

Tanya recalled a time when she had promised herself she would never be caught up in loving a man who didn't love and respect her, but it seemed that from the very first day she and Jeff were introduced, Jeff had taken a strange hold over her. He was the worst thing for her, yet she found herself drawn to him, despite his relationship with her best friend's sister.

Now, the sound of dishes and silverware clanking against one another filled the restaurant. The lunch time crowd was filing in and Tanya watched as the patrons stood waiting for an available table. The waitress, who had clearly observed Jeff leaving, cautiously approached Tanya's table.

"Ma'am has your friend left?" The waitress knowingly inquired.

"Yeah." Tanya sniffed angrily.

"I hate to do this but if you're alone I have to ask you to move to the single seats at the counter."

Tanya's red skin flushed with humiliation and her cheeks grew a deep burgundy. She avoided the waitress' eyes and looked at the people standing by the hostess booth. They were watching and waiting for her response, which added more injury to her already bruised ego. Tanya felt every eye focused on her. They all had heard and seen what had just transpired and now her private shame was public. Depressed, she grabbed her basket woven purse and hurried toward the exit.

*This is the last time I'll ever set foot in this place,* she vowed as she pushed through the door.

# Chapter Two
## Beware the Hermit

Lela stared at her laptop's screen, flustered by her lack of progress. She'd begun writing her book ten months ago and was no closer to an end than when she'd started. Although this was her third book, it was quickly becoming a meddling thorn in her side. Her days seemed endless as the pages remained blank, and this was more than writer's block; this was career suicide. She managed to creep in a few chapters here and there but nothing that moved her inwardly. Self-help books were her genre of choice, particularly those centered on spirituality, but lately she found herself searching for her own sense of purpose and could not bring herself to move forward on helping others. As she read the last few lines she had typed, she became eerily aware that her thoughts were becoming vague and uninventive.

*Life can change in a moment. This may seem like a simple concept but in reality the decision that one makes today can positively or negatively impact life for many years to come.*

Lela knew her thoughts were not original and new but they seemed to be pertinent to her own situation. Lela was independent and headstrong but her confidence was sometimes overshadowed by her fears, so instead of facing them, she wrote about them. Writing was her escape from reality and a book could be and usually was her comfort and closest friend.

Lela eased herself up in her arm chair and repositioned the laptop on her thighs. She grimaced at the sight of her thick thighs spreading as the laptop pressed down. *They're like butter,* she thought to herself, as they spread across the seat of her emerald suede lazy-chair. She pondered the idea of jumping on her treadmill for a good thirty minutes then quickly dismissed it: She had too much work to do and the treadmill wasn't going to help her write that book. She gave herself permission to relax a little and allowed her eyes to scan her cottage inspired home. Patches of papers and multi-colored legal pads covered her oblong glass coffee table, along with dozens of unnecessary pencils, more than any school age child would ever have need of. Lela chuckled at her overindulgence with writing necessities. She would never use them, but just liked the idea behind them.

*I'm a writer*, those pens and pencils announced. Ironically, they also were a bright beaming indicator that she was in the middle of a writing wasteland. Lela read over her last words again: *the decision that one makes today can… impact life for many years to come.*

She was about to put those very words into action in what she considered to be a major departure from her self-imposed seclusion. For several months Lela had been back in the Sunshine state, after leaving the rigid cold of Colorado. For seven years she had lived in the place she called her escape, until the escape became her jail. So, she returned to Cobbleville, the place she called home, in order to keep her sanity and to be closer to her aging parents, who had constantly implored her to come back home. Cobbleville was a small town rich in character and history, and only a forty minute drive to the busier streets of the state capital. So at the urging of her parents, she agreed to come back but still managed to keep her distance by building her home outside the city limits.

North Florida was a visual adventure, a masterpiece for those who thrived on three dimensional beauties. There were miles of white sandy beaches that seamlessly merged into rows of stark bristly pine trees. Ancient small tobacco row towns that appeared to have never caught up to history merged with tourist attractions that appeared larger than life. Despite all the wonderful attractions she might be missing outside her front door, Lela managed to remain hidden for months--barely revealing herself to anyone except upon request or threat by her parents.

Lela purposely avoided the busier thoroughfares of Cobbleville, hoping to keep her life, both public and private, out of the rumor mill for which the small town was known. This was very difficult to do but she managed to stay out of sight in spite of the ever increasing insistence from her parents that she attend the wedding of her high school classmates and former friends, Tristan and Jeff.

*The wedding to end all weddings,* her mother called it -- *unless Lela got married.* Lela laughed to recall her mother's attempt at subtlety.

Unexpectedly, her mother, Georgia, dropped by and interrupted Lela's day dreaming. "Are you still going to the wedding?" she asked.

"Yes..." Lela paused. "But I don't have a thing to wear." Lela observed that her mother was already dressed in a bright yellow summer suit that only Georgia could pull off. She had accented the outfit with purple stones and chunky earthy crystals that played nicely against her high yellow complexion.

"Fiddle sticks, of course you do," Georgia replied. "Don't you dare try to get out of this. Tristan really wants you to come. I don't know why you refused to be a bride's maid. You two were always so close in school."

"Things change momma." Lela continued to look at her laptop.

"Stop pretending you are working and talk to me. Why? Why did things change between the two of you?" Georgia pressed.

Lela looked up, but did not move her notebook. It was her shield, the barrier that kept her safe from nosy neighbors and her mother's inquiry.

"Momma, people grow up and grow apart... It is a fact of life. I'm sure you know this."

"Yes, but she was your best friend."

Tristan had been Lela's best friend all during high school but time, travel, and temperament had created a gap in their friendship, along with a lingering disagreement about the value of their camaraderie. Now, an hour away from the wedding of the year, Lela found herself having reservations about attending.

Her thoughts were again interrupted with a familiar chime from her laptop. Lela minimized her document to find that she had a new email from Kasuba, her college roommate, and one of the few people with whom she remained in contact.

Lela scanned the email for those all important updates that Kasuba was known to send. She was good at keeping her friends up to date as to her whereabouts and social activities. "London," Lela read out loud, then giggled. "Kasuba still doesn't know how to keep still. " She was a wanderer, the very opposite of Lela, who was a homebody. But Kasuba had been there for Lela, when no else was and could be trusted with any and all information.

Lela thought about her friendship with Kasuba and her lack of friendship with Tristan. Kasuba never stayed in one place long enough to call it home and yet Lela was always able to keep in contact with her. While Tristan had been in the same place since high school, she and Lela had not kept their friendship alive. *That's not my fault*, Lela mumbled inwardly, yet for some reason she felt guilty.

Lela quickly replied to Kasuba, wishing her safe travels and promising to send some pictures. Then, she maximized her document, hoping to write at least one sentence of some magnitude to turn her writer's block around and give her an honest reason not to attend the wedding.

While her daughter continued to ponder, Georgia had taken the liberty of going into Lela's closet to remove some clothing options for the affair, including shoes and accessories.

After a few minutes of staring into space it was clear that Lela was getting nowhere with her book, so she closed her document in defeat and placed her laptop on her coffee table, trapping some pencils beneath it.

"I guess I should get ready to go." Lela jumped up from her chair and eyed her mom, who seemed content to wait until her daughter dressed before she made her exit. However, she soon realized that Lela was not going to put on her suggested attire while she was there, so Georgia took her leave and kissed her daughter good bye.

"See you at the wedding," Georgia stated with prophetic assurance as she stepped out her daughter's front door with a wave. With those words, Lela was trapped. *There's no turning back*, she thought.

Lela knew she had a fifteen minute drive to the wedding location but she wasn't much for being punctual. The only timelines she ever had to be concerned with were the ones set by her editor, Joyce, and they were far and few between. Her newest book deal gave her some allowances with time frames of which she took full advantage but her next deadline was rapidly approaching and she still had no new ideas to send Joyce.

Forgetting about her work for a moment, Lela turned her attention to her attire. She glanced in the full length mirror hanging on her closet door. She was wearing a cement grey sweat shirt, matching pants and cozy fluffy bedroom slippers. Her sister dreads were pulled back into a pony tail, with a few stragglers settling on her face. Lela pulled the straggles back and bit her bottom lip as she flipped her closet door open and began the tedious task of rummaging through her clothes, searching for an appropriate dress to wear. With every turn of one of her wooden hangers her chest tightened and her breath began to quicken. She was in no rush to face the public and was already exhausted from the idea of having to come up with superficial small talk at the reception. She sat down on the edge of her bed and placed her head in her hands and contemplated whether she should go at all. However, she had promised her mother and Tristan that she would come, a promise she already regretted. Her chest was in full blown pain and she felt her head begin to ache. Why did she ever agree to this? She questioned her decision, but then answered herself: Because Tristan pestered her until she'd agreed.

Tristan had called Lela numerous times to make certain that Lela would attend the ceremony, but her sudden interest made Lela uneasy. It was not just Tristan's invitation but her persistent requests for her to be a central part of the wedding party. Unsure that Tristan was truly extending an olive branch,

Lela had declined the request, but still felt pressured to attend. Tristan had asked her again, reminiscing with stories of their old times together. Lela hadn't heard the 'good old days' mentioned so much as she had within the past two months, and although the sentiment was pleasant to hear and Tristan possessed a barrage of good traits, Lela was not convinced of her sincerity. She knew that Tristan had the capability to turn her charm off and on to advance her own agenda. Lela just couldn't figure out exactly what her agenda was and felt like she was being set up for something she wasn't ready for.

Lela took one last look through her closet, and then glanced at the clock on her side table. She could no longer procrastinate or she would miss the whole ceremony, so, grudgingly, she put on the dress her mother suggested, walked over to her bathroom and opened the drawer where she kept medical supplies. It was also the place least likely to be looked at by her mother during a visit. Lela grabbed a medicine bottle and removed a couple of small blue pills which she swallowed without water. She was getting too good at that, she thought, but she had no choice. She needed them, and if she didn't take them, she wouldn't make it through the wedding. As quickly as her chest pains had begun, she noticed that they were beginning to subside, but her head still ached. She pondered taking another pill, and then looked in the plastic bottle and saw that only four pills remained. *I'll save them just in case*, she thought, then made a mental note to call her doctor to request a refill. Lela put the bottle back in its place, grabbed her small hand bag and car keys and walked out the door. *Ready or not*, she thought.

# Chapter Three

## Re-Introductions

Running behind, Lela had taken a seat in the back row nearest to the exit, feeling lucky there was still a seat available. The wedding was held at a brand new country club outside of Cobbleville, and though, Lela's drive was not long; she drove at a snail's pace. Now, the crowded courtyard made Lela nervous and she assured herself that she would leave the wedding as soon as the vows were over, but for the moment she tried to settle down her anxiousness by closing her eyes while taking a deep breath. Upon opening her dark brown eyes, she was captured by the sight of a lavender blue haze that ran across the western skyline, though much of it was hidden by rubbery pine trees that were tucked in between the clouds. The trees swayed slightly under the light breeze that gave a great sense of calm to the event and was perfect for an early fall afternoon. Lela soon found herself sinking into her chair as the tension in her body faded.

The wedding party was meticulously placed, every bride's maid had her flowers and matching bracelets, and all the groom's men were wearing personalized cufflinks. Lela admired their attire; the bride's maids wore knee length soft ice blue chiffon dresses with ruffled necklines that were off the shoulder. *Very daring but smart for this weather*, Lela thought, admitting that the women seemed to carry it off well. Their necks were bare and all had their hair pulled up with gem stone earrings and matching hair pieces. The groom's men wore gray tuxes with ice blue ties and vests. Jeff was also in gray but with an ivory tie and vest.

*He must be burning up in that suit,* she giggled to herself. Although, she had to admit, the weather was not as bad as she thought it would be. When Lela first heard that the wedding was going to be outside she was certain that the northwest panhandle heat would melt everyone away. But like everything else in Tristan's life, even the climate was made to order, remarkably cool and fresh when it should have been sweltering. The meteorologist in the morning news had predicted rain for the afternoon but it seemed that fate was on Tristan's side and there was not one drop of rain in sight, which was good for her and from the look of it, good for her wedding planner, too.

Lela watched as a very high strung woman wearing sensible shoes and a two-piece black suit was running around in the background, checking flower arrangements, talking with or more like dictating to what seemed like assistants. The sensible shoe lady looked petrified at the idea that something could or would go wrong.

Settled in, Lela watched as two of her classmates declared their unyielding love for one another in front of one hundred and fifty guests. Lela waited anxiously as the ceremony dragged on for what seemed to her, was forever. Despite the threat of a slight sense of boredom, Lela generally liked weddings. It was the only social gathering she didn't mind attending -- as long as she had her trusted pills to ease her anxiety. It was more of a curiosity that brought her to weddings than her interest in the couples. For Lela, weddings were one big social experiment and it seemed that no matter what the theme was or what the cost of the affair, if the affection between the couple was genuine then the event was sure to be a love fest. And since Lela couldn't stand contrived affairs, weddings were usually the safest bet. Occasionally, she did come across some unfortunate unions, but Jeff and Tristan were putting on a convincing show for their guests.

After the vows, came a stream of candle lighting and solo performances, and to Lela, the constant movement bore a striking resemblance to a musical.

She was quickly becoming cynical but remembered that this couple had been together for over a decade and their admiration for one another had traveled to every extreme, from hopelessness to passion, from love to loathing, but they never gave up on each other. Lela decided to enjoy the remainder of the ceremony, letting a smile slowly creep to her face as she watched the two get married. *Maybe that's what real love is*, she thought.

As the official concluded the ceremony with a prayer, Lela glanced over the crowd to see if she could recognize any one from high school. She managed to spot a few other classmates, teachers and local business owners seated near Tristan's mother, Patience, who was the guru of networking. As a highly sought after entrepreneur, it was no shocker that Patience would place herself among the community dignitaries. She would never be seen sitting idly in a rocking chair gossiping her days away. Tristan's father was seated uncomfortably on the groom's side beside Jeff's mother, who appeared beaten down by time. Jeff's father was deceased, so a white rose had been placed in a chair in remembrance of the preacher.

Lela pondered the seating arrangement for a moment, considering the irony that no one could forget the bad blood between them for one evening in order to celebrate their children's union. The fallacy of the situation was outrageous, but also comical.

Lela continued her scan of the wedding guests. She admired the couples and sharply dressed elders whom she had not seen in years, knowing that more than likely she would not stay long enough to greet them that evening. Before long, her gaze was met by another's with whom she was all too familiar. Not wanting to bring attention to herself, she shifted her eyes to avoid any further stares.

"I can't believe it..." Lela whispered under her breath. As if on cue, Lela heard the honorable judge announce the newly married couple man and wife. Traditionally, the local families would be married by a minister as it was a God fearing community but if Patience had anything to do with it a judge made for better business connections for her attorney daughter.

*Great,* Lela thought and as soon as the couple had made it to the end of the aisle, she quickly dashed to greet them and almost tripped on her heels.

"Shoot," she mumbled.

Lela hated wearing heels and hoped no one had seen her fumble. As she continued to move steadily toward the couple, she practiced her remarks in her head. A step away from the newlyweds, Lela was about to open her mouth when the guarded and high-strung wedding coordinator blocked her path.

"Sorry, but you can't see them right now, they have photographs they must take."

Tristan, who had heard her planner's voice, looked in Lela's direction and got a glimpse of her old friend.

"Lela! You came." Tristan glowed in her hand beaded one-of-a-kind wedding gown. Her gown was completely traditional, with a high neckline, in contrast to her bride's maids and she was overrun with lace and gloves to match. She waived for Lela to come closer as if to announce her presence to everyone attending. Lela excused herself and slid her way past the disgruntled wedding coordinator.

"Well, I promised..." Lela smiled and hugged Tristan then turned to Jeff and greeted him. "Congratulations."

"Oh, thank you." The two chimed together as if on cue.

"Did you think this day would ever come?" Jeff added.

"It was about time." Lela responded with a slight hint of sarcasm. "Well, I just wanted to wish you well and say goodbye."

"Goodbye! Oh no... you're staying." And before Lela could make up an excuse to leave, Tristan grabbed her by the upper arm, slightly pinching into her skin and pulled her off the courtyard and inside the country club -- leaving her husband and an agitated coordinator in the dust. Lela tried to hold back, but Tristan nudged her further in. Tristan was persistent and didn't stop pulling until they were out of everyone's sight and standing in an empty hallway. Her eyes were wide with anticipation.

"So, did you see him?" Tristan asked.

Lela knew who Tristan was referring to but decided not to indulge in romantic's fantasies.

"I assume you're referring to the other half of the *J-Crew* …and the answer is no," Lela lied.

Tristan laughed at the reference to *J-Crew*. It was the nickname she and Lela had given Jeff and his friend Jake when they were in high school. Tristan's laugh was infectious, a high pitched cackle that bounced off the walls. Lela couldn't help but smile.

"You look exactly the same as you did ten years ago," Lela told her friend.

"Do I?" Tristan giggled as she twirled around in her gown. "So do you."

"You lie," Lela replied…

"No way, the only liar here is you."

Tristan peered directly into Lela eyes. "You saw him."

"So what if I did?"

Lela spotted a mirror in the hallway and moved toward it. Casually, she re-applied a clear lip gloss and dabbed her T-zone quickly with her compact cloth, her mocha brown eyes staring back at her. She had taken her locs out of the pony tail and curled the ends slightly, an affect that brought out her bronze highlights, and created a look that took her parents by surprise. It contrasted nicely with her dark chocolate skin. She looked a world away from the sweat pants-clad girl she had been earlier in the evening.

"Can you get out of the mirror and answer me?" Tristan poked Lela.

"I saw him and now I am going home."

"No. Stay."

"Don't you have pictures to take or something? Jeff is going to get really upset."

"I'm going… but he can wait …we have the rest of our lives. I haven't seen you in years."

"Well, call me. We'll go to lunch." Lela began to walk

toward the exit.

"You *have* to stay," Tristan urged. "If you don't I'll give Jake your number."

"Threats don't work." Lela laughed and kept walking. "Call me when you get back from your honeymoon."

Lela walked out the side exit and quickly made her way to the valet service booth. At times like this she wished she had played it cheap and parked her own vehicle. She remembered a time when there were no valet services in the dusty town but over the years the make-up of the local population evolved and caused a sleepy town to grow until it now included a country club. It seemed like a dream to her, that the sharecropper's grandsons and daughters now owned the land their ancestors toiled. Lela reached into her purse and found her ticket stub and then handed it to the attendant. The sun was beginning to settle and it bounced off the hoods of freshly washed cars. Feeling she had finally dodged a bullet, she began to relax.

"You're not staying?" A smooth southern tone came to Lela's ears. Although it was deeper than she had heard in a while she knew exactly who it belonged to. She could feel his voice on her back, making the hair on her neck stand on end. Lela kept her face toward the packed parking lot.

"I don't really like social gatherings," she said.

"Oh... So you're not avoiding me?"

"Avoiding..." Lela laughed half-heartedly, "You've got to be kidding?"

"Okay, I'll give you the benefit of the doubt. I do recall you liked to be home before dark."

Jake knew all too well what made Lela uneasy. She preferred to be in her comfort zone than anywhere else. She was modest and conservative with her feelings, which drove him crazy. But now that they were older he had a new found respect for her values. Jake moved to her left. Lela turned her head to see him without acting obviously curious. He was taller than she remembered; his features much more defined and almost majestic in nature. His skin was illuminated by the sun, which caused his deep pecan brown complexion to glow. He was dressed in a black suit with a checkered silver tie unraveled around his neck. In her younger days Lela had a serious weakness for Jake. She noticed how great he looked in his tux and gave her eyes permission to follow his frame before snapping them, ashamed of her indulgence.

The two had met when they were fourteen and started dating soon after. It was the longest and most significant relationship Lela had ever had, which ended with her second year into college. Jake had wanted more from Lela than she had been willing to give, and even though she had been committed to him she refused to compromise her values to keep him. She remembered their break up vividly: Jake had wanted to be intimate and she'd refused. For Lela, sex was to be shared between a husband and a wife, and in seven years her mind had not changed on that issue.

"Home is where the heart is, Jake." Lela was beginning to question where her car was.

"Yeah, I know." Jake looked over at Lela. He was astounded by her beauty, it wasn't the obvious kind. Much of Lela's appeal was more inward than outward, and she had a magnetic personality which was unusual, given her dislike of crowds. "Is it possible that you have become more beautiful?"

"Maybe," she joked.

"No maybes about it, you look wonderful."

"So do you."

"Yeah, I noticed you eyeing me during the wedding."

"I was not eyeing you," Lela countered.

"Aw." Jake laughed, then paused awkwardly. "So... you're going home?

"Yes."

"Do you *need* company?"

Lela rolled her eyes. *So, there's the old Jake,* she thought.

"No... I don't *need* company and how dare you suggest it."

"Whoa... whoa... I didn't mean..." Realizing that she had mistaken his invitation Jake stepped back. "Please don't misunderstand."

"It seemed clear to me what you were implying."

"I meant as a friend. It's been a while since we've seen each other. I thought we could catch up." He got quiet.

"Oh." Lela relaxed. "Why don't you want to stay?"

"I prefer the company of old friends over crowds." He smiled.

"Well, I suggest you go find some." Lela let out a laugh and smiled as she watched Jake's reaction. He stepped back, mimicking a shot man.

"You always did have a wicked sense of humor." Jake took a deep breath.

"Ummm, so really why don't you want to stay?" She asked.

"I just thought you and I could talk."

Lela watched as he slid his hands in his jacket pockets, thinking he looked like the young Jake, unsure of what do or what to say. "I hear you write books on spirituality. Maybe we could talk about that or share some information."

Lela was confused, since when did Jake ever care about anything remotely religious?

"Why would you want to do that?"

"Tristan, didn't tell you?"

"Tell me what?"

"I'm an ordained minister now."

Lela was speechless. No wonder Tristan was so persistent to have her attend, she probably wanted to see the look on her face when she found out. As if on cue, the valet attendant pulled up to the curb with her champagne colored vehicle, jumped out of the driver's side and circled the car to give Lela her keys.

"Sorry for the delay ma'am." The attendant said breathlessly. "I had to run all the way to the end of the lot."

Lela nodded to the attendant in acceptance of his explanation and handed him a tip for his trouble. Leaving Jake's side, she walked around the front of the car to the driver's side. Sitting in her plush leather seat she rolled down her passenger-side window. Jake stood on the curb and watched her adjust her seat and mirrors. She seemed flustered by his admission. Finally settled, she looked up to him.

"I don't think I am in the mood for company tonight ... but

congratulations."

"Thank you." He nodded his head, seeming to accept her answer.

"Do you need a ride any where?"

"No, I drove. I'll be fine."

"Well, you can't say I didn't offer."

"No I can't say that." He smiled.

Jake watched as she drove out of the country club parking lot, the sun becoming her back splash. He wondered if he should follow her but knew better than to sneak up on her like that and decided that there had to be a better approach, so he turned to go inside.

The reception hall was immaculately decorated. The fragrance of white roses and hydrangeas filled the air. Since becoming a minister, Jake had the pleasure of performing a few ceremonies, but he never attended any of the receptions, still nervous about his past image. He teetered with the idea that his old vices might reemerge if he placed himself in the wrong situation and wedding receptions had many unforeseen temptations. Single women circled like vultures and free drinks were offered at every turn, but soon he came to the realization that he was the one in control of himself and that no one could impose themselves on him if he didn't want to be imposed upon.

In reality, Jake's only real concern was his self control. It had taken him a while to learn how to balance his new life with old friends, and along the way he lost a few, including Jeff. Jake was taken by surprise when he received an invitation in the mail and had called to make sure they had not made a mistake. He soon found out that it was Tristan who'd pushed to have him invited. Since Jake was willing to repair his friendship with Jeff, he decided to make a show of peace by attending his old friend's wedding. However, it seemed that Jeff was still not interested in Jake's appearance and as he passed him in the receiving line, Jeff intentionally held back his hand from being greeted. That was the real reason Jake wanted to leave early.

Jake examined the room carefully selecting where to sit,

surprised that there was no assigned sitting. Jake spied an empty table in the corner that was so far away from anything interesting he was sure that no one would attempt to bother him. He sat facing the crowd, so that he could see if someone approached and watched the entry way. He'd hoped that Lela would change her mind about the reception and come back, but knew better than to get his hopes up.

A few other guests slowly joined his table, but he didn't know them. He cordially introduced himself, and then resumed his quiet demeanor, making himself seem as boring as possible to deter possible advancers. He was aware of his good looks, and knew they had aided him in his mischievous past.

Soon the lights fell dim and a spotlight encircled the entryway, just as the disc jockey began to announce the wedding party. Jake knew two of the groomsmen from high school and had gone to college with one of the bride's maids.

When the wedding party had taken their seats, the disc jockey started to play an old Marvin Gaye song while he introduced the bride and groom. Tristan and Jeff entered and went straight to the dance floor in the center of the room. As they danced to their first song, the photographer clicked away, as did guests who'd brought their cameras with them. Soon, the song ended, the couple rejoined the wedding party at their head table, and dinner service began. *Great*, Jake thought, *I'll get dinner, and then I'll go home.*

Lela drove at a moderate rate of speed, paying close attention to the black top road. Though there was very little traffic, the darkness of the area made it necessary to remain alert and vigilant. There weren't very many intersections, just a lot of dirt roads bordered with tall pine trees, sparse shrubbery and sandy ditches that stretched seamlessly from one county to another. The scene was tranquil and ideal for Lela's temperament. She preferred the quietness of the countryside over the bustling noise that came with living near the major cities.

Lela flicked on her high beams as she turned a narrow curve

and glided over the tar bathed slabs. The car radio was tuned to the gospel hour, one of the few local radio programs there was broadcast from the area. It didn't reach a very wide audience and usually featured news pertaining to the local grocery store discounts or church functions in between music selections. During elections, many of the citizens running for office would grace the station with their presence. This night it was relatively silent, playing one song after another, only to break for commercials. Lela looked at the time on her clock, 8:15. She wondered if she had left the wedding too early. It might have been fun, she thought, catching up with Jake. But his appearance at the wedding had caught her off guard. She hadn't expected to see him and quite frankly had managed to put his memory in the back of her mind for the last few years.

Lela's cell phone began to hum, indicating a call was coming through. She put on her hands-free ear piece and pressed the talk button.

"Hello."

"I'm glad I caught you." Joyce spoke at a fast pace.

"You act like it's not easy to get a hold of me."

"Sure it is, Honey, but I knew you were going to this wedding. Has it inspired you to write?"

To Joyce every moment in life was inspiration waiting to happen. She was Lela's first editor and she had a keen knack for motivating her writers.

"No."

"Why not? It's a wedding for heaven's sake. Love is in the air."

"My book is not about weddings, besides I really don't feel like dishing today."

"Oh, sounds like something juicy happened. Well, I'll get to it. I read your last submission… and it was ok."

"I gave you those weeks ago. Why are you just now getting back to me?"

"We had to have some people look over it, dear."

"What, what people? Why? It's not finished, you cannot properly critique an unfinished book."

"Ummm, that has some logic to it, but any way, dear, we did critique and it was just okay."

The dreaded ok. Lela knew what was coming next, a slew of revisions which meant she was going to have to do a lot more research which meant she was going to lose a lot more sleep, but it wasn't like she had slept much to begin with.

"What do I need to change?"

"Not much really, it's not what you think but a few of us were talking and I know you usually write books with a spiritual theme or revelation to them but this time..." She paused. "I think you should lay off the spiritual and focus more on the practical advice."

"Lay off?"

"What is important is that I feel that you need to incorporate more sensible ideas. You know... something tangible."

"You want me to eliminate the prayers and scriptures?"

"Yes."

"Where is this coming from? Spiritual is what I do. It's who I am as a writer. It is what I am known for."

"Yes, but we are trying to market you with a broader appeal this time."

"Uh, huh."

"You're last book did well but *I* feel that the book would have done better if it had more of a mass market appeal."

Lela became silent and she knew Joyce hated it when she got silent. It meant she was thinking too much. When Lela didn't immediately agree with her it was an indication that she was going to have to do some heavy convincing. Although, given the circumstances, Joyce understood.

"Lela. Lela, are you there?"

"I'm here."

"Well?"

"No..." she sighed.

"No."

"I can't take away the very thing that brought me success and I certainly can't put down the spiritual aspect of my writing so that I will sell a few more books."

"Ok, I get it. It's not like this is your first time around the block but think about the long term. If you cooperate with us with this, it could bring you so much money..."

"I can appreciate the practical implications of the change, I just don't agree with you on them. You're not asking me to change anyway, you're asking me to eliminate."

"Ok, you're obviously stressed. So how about you think this over, sleep on it and I'll fax you the proposed changes."

"What are some of the changes?"

"Not right now..."

"Joyce, please... you called me." Lela could hear Joyce coughing.

"We will take out all references to Jesus and make it very generic with regard to a higher power."

"I don't need to sleep on that." Lela paused. "No."

"Lela."

"No, Joyce. Tell *them* or whoever that I said no."

"Sleep on it. Have a good night." Before Lela could object any further Joyce hung up quickly. Lela turned her car into her moon lit driveway and parked by the side of her house. Turning off her engine she sat motionless and looked straight ahead at her rose bushes that were just coming into bloom. Lela noticed how the thorns seemed to line up in soldier-like formation, strategically placed around the stem that held each bloom. *I need thorns*, she thought, *people don't mess with thorns*.

Between Jake's re-appearance, his new career and her editor's phone call, Lela could feel her blood pressure rising. Lela's breath became sharp and tense as her heart seemed to quicken with every minute that passed.

"Oh, Lord help me." She began to pray. "I realize it's a test but I can't handle too much right now. I need you to intercede on my behalf, please strengthen me. I need help with my faith. I love you. In Jesus name I pray. Amen"

Lela's heart slowed to a normal pace as she felt the tightening in her chest relax, she left her car and entered her home immediately retreating to her bedroom, undressing on the way. The deep green cotton dress fell off her body landing on her bare wooden floor. She glided into her silk pajamas and slipped in her fuzzy house shoes. Feeling an urge to write, she picked up her beaded embroidered journal that lay on her nightstand. Her writing started tight and controlled but the more she mulled over the day's events the less controlled her writing became.

A minister! Lela mocked the idea that Jake had actually converted. She could hardly believe that he had crossed over to the *other-side* as he used to say to her. Although she knew she should be happy for his deliverance, she found herself jaded by it.

She remembered her own conversion; she had been sixteen, seated in the back of a packed church during a week-long revival. She was visiting her grandparents and they were devoted church goers. Lela occasionally went to church with her mother but the older she got the less it was required of her, so instead of going to church she would sleep in or hang out with Jake. Her grandparents, however, were adamant that she would attend and made no secret of their disappointment if she found a way to get out of going. So, to spare herself an argument whenever she visited her grandparents, she went.

She remembered the scent of perfume from the deaconesses and the dripping anointing oil that had been placed on her forehead during alter call, the minister always seemed to put on a little too much. It was business as usual in the church, everyone had their place. To a sixteen-year-old Lela it was a circus but somehow this time was different. The preacher was an older man, someone she had never seen before. He didn't yell or bounce around hooting and hollering like many she had seen before and he didn't wear an elaborate robe. It was just an elderly man in a pair of jeans, a button down shirt and a bible in his hand. His appearance piqued her interest, so unlike the other times she had attended service; she actually attempted to pay attention. The old man started to tell a story about a boy who was lost and didn't have a home to go to or a person in the world to lean on. Lela remembered how she had cried when the preacher told how the boy had been abused and how he had to live on the streets.

*"But there was one thing he had that no one could take from him, his faith."*

Those words stayed with her, and when it came time for alter call, Lela stood up, walked down the aisle and with two words she was born again.

*"I believe,"* she proclaimed to the minister.

*"Welcome,"* he replied.

Lela remembered how happy she had been about her new faith, only to have it discarded by the one person she loved most. Jake eventually got over it and said at the time that he loved her but once he got to college and had access to new people and more ideas, his love and acceptance faded. Lela remained determined and unwavering throughout school to the point of alienation. Her alienation caused an already fragile relationship to break even more.

"You've got to find balance child." Lela could hear her grandmother's voice. "Jesus knew how to walk his path and still love those who chose not to walk it with him. Balance child, it isn't always all or nothing."

Lela shook her head and forced herself to the present. She shuffled her way over to her living room and curled up on her oversized sofa with a bag of freshly popped popcorn and her journal. It had to be a joke, she thought, feeling new resentment.

"Jake is no minister," she hissed under her breath. She was consumed by Jake's revelation. She stopped writing for a moment and tried to reflect on her anger over the idea that Jake could have had a change of heart. *He broke my heart,* she wrote in large block letters, *how was it possible that someone who hurt me so much is now redeemed?*

Tristan stared at her new husband, while he danced with her mother on the dance floor. Dinner had been served, during which Jeff gulped down three double shots of brandy, and then immediately wanted to dance. She hated when Jeff drank, in fact, she was beginning to hate Jeff, but given that it was their wedding night and a celebration, she let it go. Tristan wasn't much for dancing; it took all the courage she had to go through with the first dance. However, Patience was rearing to go, so they abandoned the bride for the dance floor.

Tristan tried to drown out her true feelings as she watched and laughed in delight at the two, putting on her greatest show for her guests. Finally, after Jeff had worn Patience out and she took her leave, leaving a very tipsy groom on the dance floor, he was quickly joined by his groomsmen.

Tristan sipped her punch, which was now warming. Her eyes assessed Jeff's appearance. He wasn't a bad looking guy, in fact, he was actually quite handsome; but he wasn't her first choice and she knew he felt it. She pitied him, but more than that, she didn't want to be alone, while her sister stole the spotlight and her dreams.

Tristan decided to make her rounds through the crowd, thanking people for their support and attendance. She felt like she was running for county commissioner, shaking hands with everyone, taking in their well wishes.

She stopped at her sister's table and sucked her breath in sharply.

"Tristan!" Camille gushed. "How good of you to come and greet us."

Camille motioned toward her husband, Leland. Leland looked up from his plate, but joy was not brimming in his eyes. Tristan recognized that look and did her best to ignore it.

"I'm sorry it took me so long to get to ya'll but I've been kind of rushed since this morning. Not one moment to relax."

"Rushed," Leland chortled. "Sort of like this marriage."

The cynicism was clear in his tone.

"Now, now." Camille placed her hand on Leland's shoulder as if to restrain him. "How about you get my sister and me something to drink," Camille suggested to Leland.

"No, thanks. I want to be completely sober through this whole night," Leland stared at Tristan. "So no lies can be told."

Camille was sick of the little innuendos that Leland kept throwing at Tristan. She couldn't stand how Leland fussed over her sister. Granted, Leland had known Tristan far longer than he had known her and she was her husband's attorney, but their friendship was too close for anyone's comfort, especially hers.

"Well, I'll go and get my own drink then."

Camille stood and left the table. She trusted that not too much could happen in a room full of people at her sister's wedding. When Camille was safely out of hearing range, Tristan no longer held her tongue.

"What the hell is wrong with you?"

"Wrong with me? I didn't just marry someone I don't love."

"And you love my sister."

"This isn't about me, Tristan. It's about you."

"I cannot believe you are doing this at my wedding."

"You wouldn't listen to me before. You know, there is still time to change your mind."

Leland stood to face her; his closeness was unnerving to Tristan.

"I am carrying his child."

"That's no reason to be an idiot."

"Leland, why do you even care? Like I said, you sir, are married to my sister. You two have a very happy life-"

"It's not so happy," he interrupted. "You know that."

"That's not my fault. You didn't have to choose her."

"You left me know choice."

"Leland, I am not going to have this argument with you."

Her voice rose, slightly, then Tristan caught herself.

"I'm sorry." He hesitated. "O.k., Congratulations then."

"Don't say things you don't mean."

"See, there you go. I voice my opinion and you to tell me to shut up, I give in and support you, and you still shut me down."

"I don't shut you down."

"Oh, come on. You always shut me down and shut me out and that's why-"

"Why? What?" She hissed.

"Why I chose her."

"Great, Leland," Tristan uttered. "Just great. It's really nice of you to remind me at my wedding why you and I could never work." She breathed in sharply.

"I don't mean to hurt you," he said.

"Too late."

"It shouldn't matter what I think. You love him, don't you?"

"Yes." Tristan replied with more assurance than her heart was feeling.

"And you don't have any more feelings for me. I mean it's been over for years."

Leland was fishing for a sign; the one thing Tristan always did that showed that she was lying. Leland's eyes had begun to burn deep within her, stimulating emotions she didn't want to revisit, much less at her wedding. She refused to be his puppet. She suddenly spotted Jake seated at a table nearby. *Good,* she thought, *a reason to get away from Leland.*

"Enough of this!" she whispered harshly and quickly excused herself from Leland's sight, heading toward Jake, who was isolated at a corner table. The few people who had been seated there had abandoned him for the dance floor as well. Jake saw her hurriedly coming and stood to greet her.

"You look ravishing!" he exclaimed. "If I were Jeff, I wouldn't let you out of my sight."

"Ah, Jake, forever the charmer." She was still a bit nervous but she was pulling herself together quickly.

"I try." He motioned for her to sit, which she gladly did.

"I see you came alone, why no date?"

"I don't have anyone special enough to bring to a wedding."

"Ah, don't tell me that, Jake." She grinned, wondering if he had seen Lela before she left. As if he had read her thoughts, he answered.

"It's too bad Lela left right after the ceremony. She used to love to dance."

"Yeah, so you talked to her?" Tristan pried

"Yeah, I waited with her while she got her car." Jake paused. "She looks good."

Tristan noticed how reserved he was. He seemed to pick his words carefully, as if he was trying to ask something.

"So, are you going to call her?"

He looked Tristan in the eyes and laughed.

"I don't even have her number."

"What? She didn't give it to you?" Tristan knew Lela would be surprised to see Jake, but didn't think she would leave him in the lurch. He was an old friend.

"I don't think she wants anything to do with me, Tristan."

"Don't be silly, she doesn't know what she wants. Didn't you tell her you're a minister now? She should be all over you."

"Ha! I think the idea of that made her angry."

"Well, make her un-angry." Tristan smirked. "I'll give you her number, you call her."

"Great!" Jake smiled. "You can give me her address too."

Tristan cocked her head to the side and laughed. "That you'll have to pay me for; I want double for my trouble."

Jake laughed, but then looked at Tristan's stern face. She was serious.

"Look, she is going to ask how you got her information, and she'll hate me for it for a while, at least. I want compensation for the tongue lashing I am going to receive."

"How much?"

Tristan held out her hand. "Empty your pockets."

# Chapter Four
### Reunited

The hours seemed to pass quickly as Lela wrote; lost in her thoughts. She was spooked by a knock at her door. She lived in an isolated area where no one visited without first being invited. Lela cautiously looked through the peep hole of her door and much to her distress saw Jake on the other side. Immediately she craved her magic pills.

As if he could see through wood, Jake placed his palm on the door where Lela's head was now leaned. He could hear her body as it brushed against the heavy wooden door.

"Lela, open the door."

Against her will, something deep inside compelled her to open it.

Jake felt the door move and backed away. She gradually opened it a crack and stuck her head out just enough to see his face.

"How did you know where to find me?"

"We have mutual friends, remember."

"I can't believe Tristan gave you my address."

"Don't worry I had to pay her for it." Jake's attempt at a joke was lost on Lela.

"It's late, you know."

Jake looked at his watch, it was a quarter past 1:00 in the morning.

"I know… I'm sorry. I should have called first but I was afraid you wouldn't let me come by."

"You would be right. It's not decent."

A playful smile crept over Jake's face as he pondered her words. Lela observed that he was still clothed in his tux from the wedding and watched as he stuck his hands in his trouser pockets and searched for something to say.

"I think we should talk," he finally admitted.

"Don't you think it's a little inappropriate? I mean someone might misconstrue the situation and being that you're a minister, we wouldn't want that to happen." Lela bit the inside of her cheek.

"I don't know about what anyone else would think and I have learned not to care. But given that you live in the middle of nowhere I don't think that will be a problem."

Jake noticed that Lela shifted her stance, cocking her head to the side. He continued despite her obvious tense body language.

"I also don't plan on doing anything that would be disparaging to my reputation or yours." The playful smile returned.

"Reputation," Lela scrunched her face. "You have a reputation?"

"Yeah, it's one that I have worked hard to get and one I don't take lightly." His face became stern.

Lela saw that he was serious and lightened her tone as she shifted again.

"You can't stay long." Lela backed away from the door, allowing Jake to enter. The door creaked as it opened, showing its age.

Jake took a moment to admire Lela's home. It was spacious and had a warm inviting feel. The walls and floors were all wood and the smell of cedar and honeysuckle filled the air. There were lit candles in the foyer and although he had never been there before, he felt like he was coming home. As Jake stepped into the living room the floor creaked; he glanced around and observed the big stone fireplace and the large furniture that nearly overwhelmed the space. She kept her house neat but had lots of books and magazines in every corner of the house. Her back wall had a floor to ceiling bookcase filled to the brim.

"Did you write some of those?" He motioned toward the bookcase as he sat down on sofa. Lela sat in her usual seat, feet curled up.

"No. None of those are mine."

"You still write for fun I see?" Jake noticed Lela's journal sitting on the coffee table.

"Occasionally."

Jake watched as she picked up her journal and tucked it under her arm. Lela excused herself and walked into her bedroom. Upon her return Jake became aware that she had covered herself with a full-length robe and was without her journal. Lela sat back down and crossed her arms, then motioned for him to take a seat.

"So, what are you working on now?" Jake asked.

"A self-help book."

"About what?"

"Life." She smirked.

"Well... you look like you have done well for yourself?"

"I have. God has been good to me. How about you?"

Jake lifted his head. "Yeah, I've been great. I'm traveling a lot. I belong to a local church. I'm one of five associate ministers."

"That must keep you busy?"

"Yeah, it does. How are your parents?"

Jake could see that Lela was growing tiresome of the small talk and noticed her growing agitation whenever he was around.

Lela felt his eyes on her, studying her. She tried not to be rude but managed to become standoffish and she didn't like it.

Jake watched as she constantly looked away from him.

"Tell me Jake, what is it that you want?" Lela asked. She knew she was being abrupt but his presence was steadily wreaking havoc on her mental balance. Jake was the only man she ever considered putting her religion *down* for and the memories were flooding her mind as to how many times she had to resist him. Jake noticed that her body stiffened, as if preparing for an argument. Lela wore her emotions on her sleeve and could easily be read.

"I know my profession has taken you by surprise."

"Do you?"

"You resent me."

"I do?" she paused. "So, now you're a mind reader?"

"Talk to me, Lela. This will only work if you talk to me."

"What do you want me to say?" she gaffed. "You show up out of nowhere and start saying things to me like you owe me some sort of explanation and you don't."

"I think I do."

"Well, you don't. You're a grown man and you can do whatever you want with your life."

"I know that. But I know that our break-up had a huge impact on your life."

"How vain are you?" Lela couldn't believe his arrogance.

"I'm not trying to be vain."

"You're not trying hard enough. I should have known that the minister in you wouldn't change your need to be the center of everyone's attention."

Jake hung his head. He wasn't coming across as he'd hoped he would. It seemed as if the more he talked, the bigger the hole he dug under his feet.

"All I meant is... I'm sorry if I came across that way."

"So how did it happen?" Lela asked, deciding to give him a break.

"How did what happen?"

"How did you get your ordination?"

"I went to a school of divinity in Georgia."

"When?"

"Four years ago."

"Why?" she paused. "Why become a minister? You weren't content with just being saved?"

"I know it's hard to believe, given my history but I received a call from God. I had to follow it."

"It's that simple?"

"No. It's never that simple."

Lela watched Jake's eyes as he answered, "You of all people should understand."

"Why should I?" she snapped.

"Because you're supposed to be saved." Jake's eyes widened as if to plead with her to be more empathetic. "My whole family has alienated me; I didn't expect you would, too." Jake watched as Lela's mouth opened and closed, trying to respond.

"Don't you dare compare me with that pack of heathens?"

Lela's words took her by surprise as soon as they escaped her mouth. She noticed Jake shrink into the sofa as if trying to make himself disappear. She wrung her hands, regretting her comment. She was no better than they were and she knew it. At least, they had the courage to be who they wanted to be, while she hid behind walls and books, playing a role.

"I'm sorry..." she stammered, "that was uncalled for and just dead wrong, but you know what *they* say?"

"No, I don't. Tell me."

"You always hate the one you love."

"Then ...you still love me?"

Lela grabbed a pillow that was next to her and clinched it tight.

"No. I mean... I don't hate you. Of course I will always care for you." She didn't expect the conversation to take a turn. "When I saw you again it was like a memory that had aged over night. But you've changed. I was expecting a playboy and I got a minister."

"I understand."

"Do you?"

"I hurt you," he admitted. "And the very thing I hurt you for I became. Now you are torn between hating the old me and having to be nice to the new me." Jake sighed. "Okay. Maybe you don't have to be nice to me but you are compelled to be."

"I was compelled to be nice to you whether or not you were a believer."

"I know that Lela, but it's easier to hate a devil." She heard his tone soften.

"I think what bugs me the most is that you couldn't have

made this decision when we were still friends. I mean, I know we were wide-eyed but I guess I still think about what if."

"I do too..." Jake stopped and an awkward silence fell over the room. Lela watched as he tried to find the right words to say, "...but it's the past. We can move on now and forgive."

"I thought I had forgiven you until I saw you." she laughed.

"There's nothing like testing your forgiveness."

"Um..." Lela bit the inside of her cheek. "You know..." she glanced at him with haughty eyes, "you're why I am not married now."

Jake modified his position and tried to appear unfazed by her confession.

"I've dated another guy since you." Lela hated that she even mentioned it but now she would have to reveal more of herself than she was willing or even able too.

"Where was this?"

"Colorado." She spoke cautiously, and hoped that he would take her short answers as a hint that she didn't want to speak on it too much.

"Was it serious?"

"For a while..."

Jake noticed that the color in her eyes appeared to turn dark and cold as she spoke. She had drifted into other thoughts.

"Then why didn't you ...?" he started, attempting to bring her back.

Lela looked up at him, feeling as if her life was being drained from her. She recalled when she met Michael. Aesthetically, he was beyond what any young woman could hope for -- handsome, well educated and outwardly kind. Michael had offered something Jake could not -- complete acceptance of her beliefs. Yet, a broken heart and youth blinded her ability to think rationally and by the time she could see what others could see it was too late. Lela was now haunted.

"Why didn't I what?" She swallowed hard and tried to play down her building anxiety but her uncomfortable demeanor did not go unnoticed by Jake.

"Why didn't you marry him?" He tested his boundaries.

"I wasn't ready." She said flatly. The room was becoming smaller and her head began to spin.

*She's lying*, he thought. *But what was she lying about?* "You mean you were afraid," he pressed.

His words were discerning and probing and she didn't like it. Jake had changed. He was more aware then he ever had been when they were younger. He watched as Lela held her breath and contemplated her answer. Her body was tense and withdrawn. He knew he had reached a wall. Lela gathered herself enough to fake a yawn, folded her arms, then stood and walked toward the front door.

"I'm tired, Jake."

"You know, you brought this up, not me?" He didn't mean to continue to press her, but he felt compelled out of concern and maybe out of something deeper. What was this he was feeling? Jake was sure it was purely a friend caring for the well-being of someone he'd once loved. Yes, that was what it was, nothing more. Lela didn't like his digging and was going to put an end to it.

"So what if I brought it up?"

"I'm not trying to pry. I mean, I am, but." He paused, searching for the words. "I don't know what happened between you and your would-be fiancé but if you ever need someone to talk to..." He was sincere but curiosity was burning him up. Why would she mention another man to him?

"You'll be the last person I call," Lela cut him off. "I have my own friends and pastor to talk to. If, I need to talk, I'll call them."

Jake followed her to the front door, stopping just at the threshold.

"Ok, then if you won't call me, as a friend..." he paused and smiled, "Then I'll call you. I paid Tristan for your number too."

Lela tried to smile but her thoughts were still in Colorado. She watched as Jake walked down her porch steps and got in his car.

"Drive safely, Jake," she whispered.

Saved for a Season

# Chapter Five
## Time Flies

Six months had passed, yet it seemed like only five minutes had gone by since Jeff had seen Tanya. When he saw her from across the cobbled street, he realized she hadn't changed a bit, except in the hips. He could tell she had gained some weight. He watched her as she dug in her purse then put change into the parking meter. When the traffic slowed down, he jogged across the street and stopped at her side.

Tanya stood facing Jeff, a blank look on her face. She was the same though her hair was now in braids and her face was a little fuller and her skin was the same high red bone shade that he remembered. Looking at him, she appeared confused.

"What do you want?" she asked.

Tanya squinted her eyes as if she could not see the person who stood before her but knew this was no hallucination. Jeff stood in front of her, all six feet two inches of him and though more than three feet away she could smell the stench of alcohol seeping from his pores. She took note of his weathered appearance. His shirt was un-tucked and wrinkled and his eyes were blood shot and heavy with bags.

"Hey, T," he sputtered.

"It's Tanya," she reminded him, wanting to reinforce the boundaries he'd made months ago.

"Okay, sorry, Tanya."

"Again, what do you want?"

Her voice was shaky but Jeff was prepared for her attitude.

"I just saw you from across the street and wanted to say

hello. See how you were doing."

"Oh." Her voice was bitter. "Well, I don't have time to catch up with you. I'm on my way to a dentist appointment."

"Oh… maybe some other time, so…"

"I don't think so, your wife might not understand…" Tanya mumbled as she began to walk away.

"I hear you're dating Eugene now," he commented to her back. "I think that's good."

Tanya stopped a few feet away from the entrance to the dentist's office and turned to face him.

"And I hear you and your wife lost the baby…" Tanya smirked. "You don't look so good." Then, she turned and entered the building.

# Chapter Six
## Motherly Advice

"I'm coming over for the weekend." Patience declared. "I've invited some guests over to your house for dinner because I feel it's time you played hostess."

Tristan could barely believe her ears.

"You won't have to be home, I will let myself in."

*Oh crap!* Tristan thought, she had forgotten that she gave her mother a house key.

"Mom, I need to discuss this with Jeff first." She tried to interject but Patience kept right on talking.

"What's to discuss? Your mother wants to visit her family and to have a small dinner party. Jeff will understand... besides you two need visitors."

"But mom-"

"No buts, I'll see you this afternoon."

"Okay... Mom, now tell me, how did your doctor's appointment go?"

"It was okay," Patience hesitated. "I have to go back for a follow-up and to get my blood work done, but it is all normal stuff for a woman my age."

"Is something wrong?" Tristan didn't like the tone of her mother's voice.

"No, No!" Patience exclaimed nervously.

"Well, you sound weird."

"I do not! Look, everything is fine. I'll see you later." Patience hung up before Tristan could declare World War II against her.

Too busy and too tired to call her mother back, Tristan hung up her office phone and went back to reading over her latest legal brief. Her office was no bigger than a cubicle and didn't proclaim mid-level attorney, although she had diligently worked her way up through the ranks at her law firm. She was an attorney for Peterson, Lincoln and Gunner, LLP, a well recognized firm that paid her well even though her office could be described as mediocre at best.

When Tristan started at the law firm she shared a desk with two other associates fresh out of law school. The competition to get noticed by partners had been intense, but she managed to squeeze out her competitors, only to end up in a small office. At least hers had a view of the city, and with the office came a legal assistant, Madison.

Madison gingerly walked into Tristan's office with a pile of depositions and telephone messages.

"Sorry about your mother. I tried to deflect her call, but she was adamant that she speak with you." He gave her the please don't fire me look.

"It's ok, Madison." Tristan didn't feel up to reaming him and he was more than a legal secretary, he was her personal assistant and gossip watch dog for office politics. She believed in being kind to the staff – they knew about all the office politics.

"Look, you should go to lunch and so should I. So forward the phone calls to your cell, but only answer the ones from partners and court clerks. If something is really important, forward the call to my cell."

"Yes ma'am." Madison hesitated. "What about your husband?"

"Take a message." She winced at how her words sounded. What must Madison think of her?

"One more thing." Madison shifted his balance. "Leland called to confirm lunch at Sublime."

Sublime was an upscale restaurant that professionals used for business lunches, where the tab was usually picked up by the client. Tristan was supposed to be giving Leland an update on one of his commercial real estate projects but she knew he would inevitably become nosy and start to question the state of her marriage. They had spoken very little since the wedding, only when necessary business arouse, but he was adamant that they have a sit down lunch to discuss the next phase of his new business venture. In actuality, Tristan knew there was no real need for it, but Leland was still a valued client and being bossy was what he was about. He needed to feel like he was in total control of every situation and if Leland wasn't happy, no one else could be. Though it was true that a part of her heart would always care for Leland, there was no room for his and her matching egos. Something he failed to recognize.

"Okay, call Leland," Tristan told Madison. "Let him know I'll be there."

"Okay." Madison took his leave.

Sublime took up the first floor of a four-story office building. The restaurant was an open space, with room to walk between tables that were covered with white linen table cloths and centered with flowers. Modern chandeliers hung from the ceiling to give the establishment a mixture of old world glam in a new world style. It was a reservation only dining establishment for lunch and dinner, however if a VIP showed up without reservation, a patron might be asked to leave. Luckily, for Tristan, her firm and her clients had clout so she had never been so embarrassed.

Leland pulled Tristan's chair out for her, then took his seat. The two had not said much besides a usual greeting. Their waiter was prompt. Tristan ordered a glass of white wine, salmon and a small salad with dressing on the side. Leland ordered a steak medium rare, potatoes, and sweet tea. He didn't drink. In fact, when it came to his health Leland was committed to it. He didn't smoke or drink and he regularly exercised. He was the picture of an alpha male with his career goals completely in order. He had a reputation that commanded respect in the commercial real estate industry and his many other business ventures. Unlike Jeff, Leland didn't blame the world for his problems; he just attacked them and didn't like it when people got in his way.

After going over some numbers and offers from prospective buyers and sellers Tristan and Leland were served their lunches. They began to eat, silently concluding that business was over for the time being.

"How's Jeff?" Leland asked between sips of tea. However, he didn't wait for any answer. "I have a few job openings, if he would be willing to work for me. He could start tomorrow."

"That's sweet of you to offer, again, but you and I both know he won't accept a job from you."

Leland nodded his head in agreement. "Well, it's probably for the best. I would hate to have to fire him for not showing up or showing up drunk."

"Do you have to be an ass about it?"

"I'm just stating a fact."

"I am not going to go through this with you all the time, and I would appreciate it if you would stop bashing my husband. You don't see me constantly belittling your wife's character, and you know there is plenty I could say."

"Yeah, so say it." Leland leaned back in his chair. "I know that everything you'd say would be true, so what? If you hate her, say it. If you think she is self-absorbed and vain, say it, but it won't change the fact that I married her and you married *Mr. Wonderful*."

"What a pair we make." Tristan frowned. "Unhappy, in love with the wrong people, and we don't know how to fix it."

"Well…" Leland chewed on a piece of steak. "We could fix it by divorcing, but neither of us likes to be called a quitter or a failure. Or…" Leland smiled cryptically, "…we could have an affair."

His eyebrow was raised in anticipation of Tristan's negative comeback, but deep within he hoped for a sign in the affirmative.

Tristan sat silently, she hated when he did this. Run! Her moral compass screamed with frustration as her frown grew deeper. Leland noticed her unpleasant glare and cleared his throat.

"Now, don't freak out, woman. I'm just joking."

"Are you?"

Tristan knew better. Leland was a fisherman; he threw out an idea like bait on a hook just to see if he would get a bite, and if she had shown just one sign of a willingness to test the waters, she knew very well he would dive right in and go for a swim.

"O.k. you know me too well." He finally gave in. "Look, I am going insane with this woman."

"That woman is my sister and your wife and as much as I cannot stand her, she is still *my* sister and *your* wife."

"Okay… Okay… you're right, and I know it."

"Promise me you won't cheat on her. If you get to that point just leave, ask her for the divorce, but don't cheat on her."

Leland pondered the request for a while, and sipped on his tea. "Are you sure that is what she would want?"

"No, I am not sure. Some women are willing to sit back and let their men do whatever they want as long as they don't leave. But don't you think she deserves better than that?"

"Well, she is a great mother, and she was there for me in the beginning."

"That says a lot. Maybe you two should try counseling."

"Counseling?" Leland huffed. "I don't need to spill my guts to some quack that is going to charge me an arm and a leg for one hour and then tell me everything that I do wrong."

"Well, better some quack, than me." Tristan laughed then straightened her face, "Because I am certainly billing you time and a half, for this ridiculous hour."

Her mother beat her home. Fortunately for Tristan, Jeff hadn't made it home from his job search yet. Tristan had not told Jeff that her mother was coming to visit or that she had given Patience an extra key to their home. She wondered why she was allowing her mother to impose on her life so much. It was beyond belief to her siblings, Eugene and Camille. However, Tristan knew something that they did not: In spite of the wonderful wedding and their ten years of dating, she and Jeff were having difficulties adjusting to married life. This was something she didn't want to admit to her family, but was willing to admit to Leland because their friendship predated Jeff.

Jeff and Tristan were under considerable strain from the start and fighting constantly. The two had looked forward to the baby, but within a month of their new life together, Tristan informed Jeff that she had miscarried.

Jeff took the loss much harder than Tristan could ever have anticipated and began to act out. Soon after, he lost his job with the airport. Money, however, was not yet an issue. Tristan tried to balance her home and career but soon her ambition to become partner outweighed her duty to be a wife. She spent more time at work than at home, and even while at home she spent the majority of her time in her home office. The only time the couple did not argue was when they were making love -- but those moments had become few and far between.

The argument was always the same. Jeff felt the need to be more of a provider and despite Tristan's support, he struggled with the idea of not being able to bring any income into their home. It was a classic concern between many couples, but a problem Tristan had never felt that she should have to deal with, given the fact that Jeff always knew what career Tristan was going to pursue. Tristan thought about their argument before she left for work. It was the same as it always was.

"You said you would to support me and my career." Tristan watched him as he ate his breakfast. Jeff wolfed it down, barely chewing.

"I do want to support you." He guzzled some orange juice. "I just think I should make more of a contribution to our bills."

"But you do contribute."

"How? You pay the mortgage and the utility bills. I don't get a say in anything around here. And because you control the purse strings, you make all the decisions. If you feel like rearranging or buying something you just do it. You don't consult with me. Why? I'll tell you why. Because you don't think you should have to consult with me about *your* money."

"I don't know what you're talking about."

"Of course you don't."

"Well, if you really want to help, maybe you should keep a job," she mumbled.

"What?" He stood up from the table. Tristan looked him sternly in the eye.

"I don't mean anything by it. It's just that... well." She sighed. "I spoke with Leland, and he said he has a few positions available if you're interested."

"You spoke to Leland, about me. Why would you do that?"

"He's family. And he's willing to help."

"I bet he is. Willing to help himself to you."

"That's not true." However, she knew it *was* true.

"Whatever, Tristan. I don't need your help or his help to find a job. I'll do it on my own and you should be ashamed of yourself..."

"What is that supposed to mean?"

"I told you never to talk to him."

"He happens to be one of my best clients and one of the reasons I am on track to be made a partner at my firm. Besides he's my friend and my sister's husband."

"A sister you can't stand because she married him and you didn't! You got stuck with me."

"I cannot believe how you are acting right now."

"I'm out of here."

It was the same argument every morning and it was the same argument they'd had before they got married. Her mother had warned her not to move in with Jeff before they got married, and of course, Patience referred to it as *shacking up*. Tristan didn't see any harm it. She was sure that once she and Jeff shared a home together all the problems they had would disappear, and if not then, they would certainly diminish once they were married. She prayed that everything would fall into place and that she would learn to love Jeff.

She prayed that her secret wouldn't have any lingering effects but it did. One lie, led to two, then three. Before long, the only way to get out of her continual story telling was to make up an even more horrific story, but she hadn't counted on her fictitious words having such a messy and lingering after effect.

She was left with two choices: Try to preserve her marriage or abandon it, and to date, it would seem to outsiders that she was ignoring her sinking boat. Jeff was distant and he knew that Tristan was keeping something from him but instead of pressing the issue, he clung to the fear that if his suspicion was wrong, he would lose her; or that if he were to press her, she would in turn bear down on him and his not-so-secret affair with Tanya would be exposed.

Tristan entered the house through the garage door, cell phone in hand as she had just finished a conversation with her legal secretary. Although the traditional work day was supposed to be over, she still had a few briefs to look over before tonight's dinner. She wanted to avoid her mother until she could get the work finished and wipe the restless look off of her face. Patience had a way of knowing whenever her daughter was upset.

As quietly as she could, Tristan crept to her office and turned on her computer to check her email for the eleventh time that day. She glanced over the new entries, and immediately recognized an email that was out of place. The addressee was Tanya! Tristan reviewed the cursory information to see if it had a subject, but none was indicated.

"What could she want?" she whispered under her breath as she glanced at her watch. *I don't have time for crazy junk mail*, she thought.

In all the years that they had known each other, Tanya had never really communicated with Tristan except for an occasional hello, even though Tristan new that Tanya and her brother, Eugene, were dating. Tristan clicked on the 'read' icon just as Patience trotted into the office holding a coffee cup wrapped in a small hand towel to protect her hands from the heat.

"You're home?"

Tristan didn't answer the obvious, just kept her eyes on the screen.

"You're working again?" Patience persisted.

"Something like that."

"But you just got home…"

"Work doesn't stop just because I leave the office."

"It should, it's after seven." Patience watched as her daughter ignored her. "You know that your work could be alienating your husband. That's probably why he's not home."

"That's his problem."

"No that's your problem," Patience insisted. She continued to watch her daughter. Seeing Tristan fail at marriage saddened her. Patience felt responsible for every misstep her children made, taking them as a direct result of her own mistakes. She didn't always show her concern in the most understanding way, and not wanting to continue the tone of the conversation, Patience changed the subject.

"You need to go to the salon and do something about your hair."

"What?"

"This is the type of stuff I'm talking about. You have to keep yourself up for your man." Patience kept rambling.

"I do keep myself up. You just caught me on a bad week."

Patience sipped her coffee, allowing the aroma to fill her nostrils. She worried about her daughter's marriage, which was slowly coming apart from the seams. This made her look bad.

"Why don't you take a break? You are a married woman now, and you should be preparing dinner for your husband."

"So, I should take a break to fix Jeff dinner."

"You know what I mean."

"No mom, I don't. Please tell me again why I am a horrible wife."

Patience glanced over her daughter's shoulder and tried to get a peek at the computer screen.

"You're not a horrible wife but there are things about marriage you don't yet understand and I am trying to help you."

Tristan shuddered. Her mother had a way of cutting her down as if her words shouldn't bother her.

"Fine." Tristan closed her email without reading the letter

from Tanya

and turned to face her mother.

"Please share with me all of your wisdom."

"You don't have to be sarcastic."

"No. No. Please, I really want to know from the all-mighty divorced one, what it takes to keep a marriage going."

Patience's face fell. She had divorced Tristan's father after the children were out of the house and well established, but the affect was no less grave on her adult children. None of her three children knew the full story behind the break-up and none had bothered to ask for details. Patience swallowed her coffee slowly, and allowed her daughter's words to sink in. She nodded her head in momentary defeat, then straightened up and looked Tristan in the eye.

"You're trying to shift the subject and I am trying to keep you from making the same mistakes I made. My failure doesn't have to be your failure."

"You don't have to get into this with me. So spare me." Tristan huffed.

Patience's eyes grew wide. Opinions she could take, lack of respect she could not. "You have already crossed the line of disrespect. You'd do well to apologize."

"I'm sorry." Tristan knew she had gone too far.

"Fine." Patience paused and her voice softened. "Tristan."

Her daughter looked up at her from where she sat.

"Right now, you're holding your marriage with one hand and you need to hold it with both hands." She sighed, then rolled her eyes. "Besides, you should take better care of your husband ... you have an image to uphold."

Tristan chuckled to herself; once again, Patience's good advice is over shadowed by her ever emerging ego. Tristan stood up to stretch the tension away that had gathered in the center of her spine and ran her fingers through her shoulder-length hair. Her mother was right about one thing, she needed to get her hair done but how her hair affected Patience was beyond her.

Tristan walked toward the hall and stopped in front of a full length mirror. She eyed her body and realized she had gained a few more pounds. The evidence was all over her stomach. Her dress slacks had begun to pinch her mid-section. She resented her mother's comments about her appearance. Tristan could still see her mother from where she stood. Patience had left the office and crossed over to the brightly lit living room and placed herself on the navy love seat.

"Catherine Sutter called me while you were out."

Catherine Sutter owned a travel agency in town, off the main stretch of road and was the ultimate gossip queen. Patience's curious tone indicated to Tristan that something was coming.

"Oh, really? How is Ms. Sutter?" Her voice carried into the living room.

"She's fine. It's a funny thing. She said she saw Tanya talking to Jeff on the street."

Tristan rolled her eyes and looked back at her reflection in the mirror. "Really momma, what else did she say?"

"Well, she was wondering if you two were having problems and you know I can't stand gossip."

In the short time her mother had been in her home she had managed to insult Tristan as a wife and was now inferring that her husband was having an affair with her brother's girlfriend.

"You know what mom? I truly mean no disrespect but you're beginning to get on my nerves. You know as well as I do that Tanya is seeing Eugene."

"I never liked that girl."

"So, you're trying to find a reason to disparage her?"

"No! I'm just trying to help."

"Well, don't. You haven't called Eugene with this mess have you?"

"Of course not. I wouldn't bug him with mindless gossip."

"But you'll bug me."

"*Don't get sassy. You're not so grown that you can't get a whipping.*"

"Whipping? What does she think this is?" Tristan chuckled under her breath.

"I heard that. You would do well to listen to my advice,

Tristan. From what Ms. Sutter told me Jeff has been at the bar a lot. Now, listen," Patience commanded. "He doesn't have a job. Unemployed and drunk don't make for a good or happy man. If you two aren't going to make it, there may still be time to get this thing annulled."

Tristan tried to pay no attention to her mother as she looked in the mirror. Her face was hardened and now more than ever she resembled her father. She had her mother's wide almond shaped brown eyes but she was an exact replica of her father. When Tristan was little, Patience used to call her the color of the earth. She remembered Patience explaining the differences in complexions. Tristan was often teased because of her darker skin but Patience made sure she learned how to appreciate her beauty.

"Baby, we're all made in God's image and he made us all the colors of the earth. We're connected, whether we're the color of acorns, deep soil, dandelions, or red clay."

Tristan missed that side of her mother, the nurturing side. About the time Tristan turned eighteen her mother started criticizing her and hadn't let up since.

In order to escape her mother's constant critique, Tristan started dating Jeff. Jeff didn't seem to mind her weight or care about what she looked like and he made sure to compliment her all the time, something she never got from her own father. Being voluptuous could bring both good and bad attention and she had her share of both.

"Tristan!"

Tristan jumped as her thoughts were interrupted by Patience's shrieking voice.

"Yes mama."

"Don't you hear me calling you? You've been ignoring me this whole time."

"Mama..."

"It doesn't matter anyway. Lela is on the phone."

Patience's voice projected from the living room. Tristan was so immersed in her thoughts she didn't even hear the phone ring.

"I'll take it in the kitchen." Tristan hurried to the phone in an effort to avoid any further conversation with her mother and in the kitchen she would be out of hearing range.

"He hasn't called at all," Lela jokingly whimpered.

"Maybe he is working up the nerve."

Since the wedding Lela and Tristan had spoken regularly and developed a new camaraderie. It was something that Tristan truly appreciated and since Lela's closet friend was constantly traveling, it became a relationship that she herself found she had missed and desired.

"I can't believe he shows up after all this time, comes to my home unannounced and uninvited, gets me all riled up and then doesn't call for months."

"Call him."

"Why'd you give him my number anyway?" Lela ignored Tristan's suggestion.

"Because you two were meant for each other, always have been." Tristan laughed, "And because he paid me forty bucks, so call him."

"You owe me forty bucks." Lela laughed. "Besides, he came looking for me. If he wants to talk to me, he should call me."

"Same old Lela. Your way or no way."

"That's right," Lela agreed.

"I was being facetious."

"Yes, I know. But you are still right."

"So, you want to talk to him?"

Tristan hoped that Lela and Jake would rekindle their relationship but more than anything she hoped that Jake's new disposition would rub off on Jeff. Her husband and Jake had been at odds for a few years and Tristan never understood what happened between them.

"It's just not that easy, Tristan."

"What's difficult about it? You like him. I know he likes you."

"What makes you say that?"

"Lela, he showed up to your house at one in the morning just so you two could talk and work out the past. And now you are going on and on about him not calling you."

"That doesn't mean anything."

"My black butt, it doesn't mean anything."

"Um, okay." Lela chuckled. "Okay, so I may have some interest in being friends with him again, but *just* friends."

"Just friends," Tristan yelped. "Ha!"

"Besides, I sort of pushed him away."

"Pushed him away? You couldn't push that man away even if you really wanted to."

"I could."

"I don't think so, he's stubborn. Always has been."

"So what?"

"So… he's not easily broken down. He'll put up some crazy guerrilla warfare on your butt."

"Well, I know how to handle him."

"Ummmm, I don't think you are as willing to keep him away as you are putting on, or you wouldn't be so concerned that he hasn't called."

"I'm not concerned. I just find it silly that he did what he did and then doesn't bother to call."

"Well, you said you pushed him away, so what did he do to get the royal boot?"

"He was getting too personal with the questions, so I told him I was tired."

"You, my dear, need a man."

"I don't need a man."

Tristan heard the animosity in Lela's voice and knew she had touched a nerve.

"I'm sorry. I didn't mean to insult your ability to remain single and perfectly happy."

"Okay, fine. Change of subject. What's going on with you? How's Jeff?"

Tristan replayed the question in her mind. *How is Jeff?* she pondered. *Fine, he's fine. No, the hell he isn't.*

"Why did I ever marry him?" She finally caved.

Lela knew that Tristan and Jeff had had a few disagreements since the wedding, but didn't think that Tristan regretted the marriage. Wasn't it normal for newly married couple to go through a learning curve at the beginning of a marriage?

"Because he was cute," Lela kidded, hoping it would ease Tristan's mind.

"Funny."

"You two have known each other for years. If you hurt, he hurts. Was there ever any doubt that you two would end up together? I mean, it takes time to get used to each other in this new capacity."

"Yeah, but there was doubt about whether we could seriously make a go of it." Tristan paused. "We weren't ready for this. I was stupid to say yes to him."

"Well, you're in it now so you should try and work your problems out."

As Lela spoke the words, she didn't really know if she believed in them, but she wasn't going to encourage Tristan to end her marriage. Lela believed in the vows people took to commit one to another. She hoped to take those vows one day but wondered if she would ever be emotionally ready for that step. It was silly of her to think about Jake when she couldn't even be near a man without feeling trapped, but she was lonely and the lonesomeness was beginning to edge into every part of her life, including her work.

"I think he is seeing someone else," Tristan said, going on to tell Lela what her mother had said.

Tristan's words cut into Lela's thoughts. *Not this again.*

"So, because your mother said that some meddlesome woman saw your husband talking to someone else on a *public* street, now you believe he is having an affair."

"No..." she lied.

Lela knew that Patience's opinion weighed heavily on Tristan's decisions. Tristan went to college where her mother went to school and went to law school because her mother had believed it would be a good profession. The only subject that Tristan ever rebelled against her mother was with Jeff. Patience never liked him because he didn't fit into the family image that she wanted for her daughter.

"So, why do you think he's cheating?"

"I don't know … but something doesn't feel right."

Tristan was too embarrassed to tell Lela that he had been staying out late and coming home smelling of alcohol and perfume.

"You're newlyweds. You need time to work out the kinks in your relationship."

"We've known each other for years, what kinks?"

"Just because you dated for half your lives doesn't mean you knew each others' every habit."

"Fiddle-sticks." Tristan pouted. Something else worried her and Lela could hear it in her voice.

"What?" Lela probed.

Tristan hesitated… "I took a pregnancy test this morning."

"And?"

"I'm pregnant." Tristan's face fell into a frown as she crunched her nose, then repositioned the phone on her shoulder.

"Is that a bad thing?"

"No."

"Uh huh… So?"

"I guess a baby is a good thing but we're not in a stable place right now."

"Baby's are always good things. It's the parents that can be messed up."

Tristan contemplated the comment and questioned whether it was a reflection on her.

"Have you told Jeff about the pregnancy test?" Lela asked.

"No, I haven't had a chance."

"Haven't had the chance but you found out this morning."

"Actually, I've known for a week."

"What happened this morning?" Lela asked.

"I took a pregnancy test this morning just to make sure."

"What did you do a week ago?"

"I went to the doctor." Tristan pouted.

"So, you thought the doctor might be wrong?" Lela tried not to giggle but failed. It always amazed her at how daft her friend could be.

"They make mistakes, besides I just wanted to be sure." Tristan was more concerned about Jeff's reaction to her pregnancy and whether it would bring out any resentment, but soon she was going to have to face him.

"Well, you might want to fill Jeff in on this little detail." Lela continued chuckling.

"Stop laughing at me. I'll tell him tonight." Tristan sighed. "What about you? Are you going to call Jake or what?"

"Or what?"

"Lela! Someone has to take the first step and I think he already did. So, stop being a juvenile and call the man."

Saved for a Season

# Chapter Seven
## Unspoken Words

♫ *It's never too late to try again...* ♫ The radio crooned softly from the kitchen and the words were beginning to cut into Tristan's thoughts. ♫ *It's never too late for a new beginning. He won't leave you alone. Just call on him, he will never leave you.* ♫ Tristan was a growing skeptic but the song repeated its persistent chanting. She could hear her mother in the kitchen humming to the music while she cooked dinner. Patience had planned a dinner party without Tristan's permission. Tristan immediately grew weak when her mother informed her that she had invited dinner guests but there was no time to call it off as Jeff was in their bedroom grumbling about the unwelcome interference.

Tristan entered cautiously, standing in silence at the foot of the bed, watching Jeff's back as he looked through the closet for clothes to wear.

"We have to talk." Tristan's voice was pensive and Jeff could tell she was nervous.

"What's wrong?"

"Nothing is wrong... I mean not really."

*A baby was a good thing,* she kept repeating in her head as Jeff rummaged through his shirts. Finally, he settled on one and pulled it off a hanger.

"I'm pregnant."

"As in, with a child?" Jeff stopped buttoning his shirt to look at his wife.

"Yes."

She watched him as he contemplated his reply. Jeff tried to

look at her and get a read on how she was feeling but he couldn't tell. She was distant... hiding her feelings. She did that well. Since the miscarriage the idea of another lost pregnancy haunted him but to him it seemed that the idea of another failed pregnancy did not worry Tristan as much; which caught him off guard. She didn't mourn the loss as much as he did, so much so, that he wondered if she really cared. Whenever he tried to talk about it, she would put him at arm's length. In any regard, as a result he didn't know how to react to the news.

"That's wonderful." A tight grin spread over his face. "Baby, that's fantastic. I told you we could get pregnant again." He was cautious.

"You're not mad?" She was pensive.

"Why would I be mad? We can finally start our family!" Jeff exclaimed, "This is great news."

Although he seemed happy Tristan knew he was keeping something from her and it made her uneasy. However, she was satisfied at the moment but her mother's earlier comments were still nagging her.

"My mom told me that Ms. Sutter saw you in town today."

Jeff stiffened.

"Really? Where?"

"Near my dentist's office. She said you were talking to Tanya."

"Yeah, she needed change for a parking meter."

"Did you help her?"

"Yeah."

"Are you sure that's all you did?"

"Yeah, baby that's all." Jeff reached for Tristan and brought her close to him. "What's this about?"

The smell of mints and alcohol floated from his mouth. It was an all too common occurrence and Tristan was becoming used to it. However, she didn't want to mention it even though Jeff could tell she was unnerved.

"Look, I know it hasn't been easy for us these past few weeks but we are going to make it better between us. I got a job today."

"That's great. Where?"

"The shop with Mr. Wilken."

Mr. Wilken was a friend of the family and a former business partner of Tristan's father. She was more surprised than pleased that Jeff had found work, and hoped it would distract him from so much heavy drinking. However, despite Jeff's assurance that everything was fine Tristan couldn't help but think that he was unhappy. Her parents had been married for twenty-five years when they divorced and she knew how simple it could be for any man, much less her father, to give into his temptations when his home life was not living up to expectations. But she prayed this wasn't the case for Jeff.

"Tristan, come help me." Patience's voice traveled from the kitchen to their bedroom. Jeff gently strokes his wife's face with his thumbs, kissed Tristan on the forehead, and then again on the lips. For a brief moment, the uneasy feeling that had plagued Tristan disappeared, but it quickly returned when she tasted the remnants of his day of drinking. She hastily pulled away.

"What's wrong?" he asked.

"You've been drinking."

"So what? I'm a grown man. Why you always trying to start an argument?"

"I'm not. Stop being so defensive."

"You can't ever just be happy."

"Baby, I can... I just." Tristan fumbled on her words.

"Go help your ma." Jeff cut her off and she watched as he turned his back to her. She noticed how he had become more abrupt and aggressive toward her. What would be a small disagreement with other couples started a war with Jeff. It made her afraid to talk to him about anything. She didn't want to push the issue, so she left her husband's side and rejoined her mother in the kitchen. If how he spoke to her now was any indication of the future, she was going to be in for a long haul and she didn't have the energy to continue the same argument for the rest of their lives, especially now that she was expecting.

Lela found it enjoyable to sit on her porch and write despite the fluctuating weather. The past few weeks were filled with either a monsoon of rain fall or an uncomfortable drop in temperature. This day was no different. The evening sun was quickly being overshadowed by large clouds and a brisk wind threatened to blow Lela's freshly blooming lilies right out of the ground. From her covered entrance she had an expanded view of her property, which began with a massive willow tree at the entrance. The driveway was a mixture of red clay and sandy soil native to the area; the path was lined with green grass moist from the day's humidity. The driveway extended past her home and encircled the rustic homestead.

Lela had worked hard to buy her home. She had started out as a copy writer for a small newspaper, and then transitioned into freelancing for magazines and blogging about any and every topic on the internet. After many phone calls and mailing out queries she found an agent who was willing to take a chance and within two weeks she sold her first manuscript. It was a historic and triumphant achievement for her. The advance wasn't much, but it was enough money for her to gain confidence in her craft.

There had been many times when she questioned whether writing was a talent she actually possessed, but after a bunch of odd jobs and trying and failing at other careers she figured if she was going to be broke she was going to be broke doing what she loved.

In the past, Lela had chosen her careers more out of curiosity and survival than natural ability or love. She tried dog walking, fast food, custodial, secretarial, librarian, selling cosmetics, energy drinks, bartending, and her favorite was when she worked for the local television news as a product tester. Everything she loved she was able to keep. Yet, writing was where her heart was and where she was most diligent. But lately, she had become uneasy with writing about God. She could see her faith waning but didn't know how to stop it. There she was, getting ready to produce another book to educate others on how to better love God, and she steadily pulling away from God.

*You're a fraud* she thought. Fear struck her hard and she felt dizzy. She breathed deeply, controlling her breath.

Lela heard a car approaching, and watched as a thick dust rose from the entrance of her driveway, which was a quarter of a mile from her porch steps. Splatters of flying clay dropped from the rotating wheels that inched closer to her. She watched as dust followed the black sedan, forming a ring of burnt orange on the car's lower half. The car came to a stop parallel to where she sat. Lela's breath was now under control and she was more curious about who her visitor could be. She attempted to look inside the sedan windows, but the tint made it difficult to see clearly. The only thing she knew for sure was that the figure inside was plainly male.

Suddenly, Jake exited his car and leaned over the hood.

"Good afternoon." He smiled. Lela noticed that he was holding a package.

"You mean good evening."

"Oh, yeah it is getting late." Jake smiled.

"It seems you have a habit of showing up to my house unannounced."

"Do you want me to leave?"

Lela ignored his question and eyed his vehicle.

"You're going to have to wash your car."

Jake looked at the dirt that now covered his wheels.

"I'll take it as a souvenir." He smiled, and noticed that she hadn't moved from her spot. "Speaking of souvenirs, I have something for you." He looked down at the package.

"What's that?"

"Well, I've been making my rounds... I was asked to speak at some functions out-of-state, so I have been traveling nonstop for the past two months. But I was thinking of you."

"You where thinking of me?"

"Oh, yeah."

"Then you should have called," she said flatly.

"I'm sorry. I didn't realize you cared." He rubbed the back if his neck, grinning.

"I don't."

"Really? Well, this will be a short visit then." He watched her as she shifted her stance nervously. "May I come in?"

"I don't care... I really don't." She paused, "But if you promise not to pry into my personal life, you can come in."

Jake made his way up the stairs and stood face-to-face with Lela. She felt her temperature rise from the close proximity and again Jake watched as she hung her head as if to yield.

"I make no promises, but I will cook you dinner if you let me." His smile was cryptic.

"Don't look so happy, Jake." Lela motioned for him to join her.

"Why are you sitting outside in this weather? You're going to get sick."

"You mean you're going to get sick. You never could take any cold weather."

"Hey, I can take cold weather." He laughed.

"Right." Lela joined him in laughter. "So are you going to make me ask you again?" She motioned toward the package.

"Oh." Jake laughed, "I almost forgot." He lied. Jake never forgot anything. He handed the small package to Lela. "Open it."

The package was small but heavy and wrapped in brown paper. Lela lifted the box to her nose and smelled the wrapper; she loved the aged aroma of casing paper. She then carefully removed the paper to reveal a carved wooden cedar box. Lela admired the craftsmanship, and then opened the container to reveal a small bronze statuette of a young woman sitting on a stump reading. She was wearing glasses and held a quizzical grin on her face, her eyes fixed on the pages of her untitled book.

"I saw it..." he paused, "and I immediately thought of you."

Lela smiled at the gesture. *He thinks he knows me*, she thought. "Thanks. It's very sweet."

"You're welcome." he beamed. "My mom has been dying to talk to you. I told her that you were back and that you live right outside of town."

"You told your mother?" Lela sighed.

"She always loved you."

"I know, but really." She didn't want the world knowing she was here.

"It wouldn't hurt you to be more social. There are people who care about you."

"Again, I know that."

"Do you? Because you act as if everyone is out to hurt you."

"I do not," Lela stammered. "And just because I appreciate my privacy doesn't mean that I'm being anti-social."

"What reason would you have to lock yourself away from the world like this?" He was getting personal yet again and it bugged her.

"I have my reasons and they're none of your business! If you are going to continue to dig, then you can leave. My life is my own."

"Okay." he retreated. "Your life is your own."

"Thank you. Besides, you're the one who stayed away for months, not me."

Lela watched as Jake sat silently, rubbing the back of his head with his palm. *He's anxious*, she thought. She took her eyes off of him and turned in time to see some clouds part and catch a peek of the sun setting. The trees on the lawn were swaying from the night wind as it began to pick up steam. The two sat in silence and enjoyed the moment. Jake had learned to admire and be more in awe of nature from Lela. She had taught him how to be in the moment, instead of trying to create one -- something he didn't always appreciate when they were younger. His current transformation did not go unnoticed.

Even as they sat together, Jake fidgeted with his hands. He didn't want to ruin the moment by saying something stupid, but he also didn't want to miss his chance to ask Lela what he'd come there to ask.

"I would appreciate it if you came to church with me this Sunday." His voice interrupted the quietness.

"Okay."

*Okay*, he thought. That was too easy. But he knew Lela was happy to be invited, even though she tried not to show her enthusiasm. He looked over at her, taking in her beauty. The moon had risen, causing a night glow to light up her face. In that moment he saw a younger Lela, the one who would tease him with her eyes. All at once, he found himself caught up in a moment and wanted desperately to tell her how he felt. Jake swallowed hard trying to push the nervousness back down to his stomach.

"I've missed you," he blurted.

Lela became flushed and her heart quickened as she bit the inside of her cheek not knowing how she should respond or even if she should respond at all.

"I mean... since I saw you last all I could think about was you. It was almost distracting and I can't afford to be distracted ... or at least I thought I couldn't afford to be." Jake took a deep breath.

"I've missed you, too," she interrupted, not wanting him to feel like he was alone. Jake took her hands in his and held them loosely.

"God and my ministry are my first priorities right now."

"I understand."

"I stayed away because I didn't know what we had started, if we had started anything."

Lela squeezed Jake's hands, and with a mellow and declarative voice reassured him again.

"I understand, Jake. At first, I was really confused by the fact that you didn't call, but after thinking about it and seeing you now, I really do understand."

Jake breathed a sigh of relief.

"Well, now that we have that over with we can move on from here."

"Move where, Jake? You and I have some issues to work out."

She still didn't know where she wanted their friendship to go and she certainly didn't know what exactly he wanted from her. She needed clarification.

"What issues? I was a jerk in the past and fortunately I have gone through a major change. I would like to think that I'm not a jerk anymore.  So, if you would… forgive me and understand that who I am now is real.  Lela, this is no false conversion."

"I don't doubt your faith."

"So many people do."

"I'm not those people."

"I need your support."

"Did you come back here just because you needed someone to support you?"

"No, of course not… but that is one aspect."

"If you want someone to be around whenever you call, then get a dog."

"Lela, you can't be serious."

"You're telling me that in four years there was no one else you could find that would support you?   Women throw themselves at men like you."

"I didn't need or want some random woman.  I wanted you."

Lela was having a hard time believing that he had not slipped up in four years, despite his apparent sincerity.

"I just don't know if I should completely trust you."

"I can see that."   Jake rubbed the back of his head again. "Tell me Lela what is it that you want?  Should I be trying to rekindle this relationship?"

"Is that what you're trying to do?  Whatever happened to just being friends?"

"Maybe I'm not making myself clear, but that's what I want."

"You have responsibilities now and your first priority has to be your commitment to God. Remember, you just said that."

"I know what I just said and I'm not changing tunes.  But love is not limited.  I should be able to serve God and have a family too."

"Family? Whoa."

"Wait… wait… don't get spastic on me.  I wasn't talking about wanting a family today." He leaned backed and allowed his head to rest against the exterior of the house.  "I feel like I'm chasing memories."

"Not our memories. You know they aren't the best to chase."

"They weren't all bad, in fact, they were mostly good, no great," Jake said.

Lela breathed a sigh of admittance. He was right. Up until the last few months of their relationship it had been mostly good times, the best of times. But she knew that sometimes loneliness could take over common sense.

"Even if that is true, we broke up for a reason." *Good*, she thought, *that will let him know where I stand.*

"You know what I mean," Jake tried to counter.

"Spare me, Jake. All you wanted when we were younger was sex and when I wouldn't give in, you left the first chance you got. It's kind of hard for me to believe those traits are totally purged from your system."

"I messed up a lot but I was foolish then. I've learned from those mistakes. I've abstained from sex since my conversion and I haven't looked back."

"You haven't slipped up once?"

"No." He rubbed the back of his head again, as he searched for the right words to say. "Don't get me wrong I'm not going to say it has been easy. It was hard at times but I have learned not to put myself in tempting situations."

Jake watched as Lela nodded her head in agreement. She didn't know why she was being so hard on him, but his words reminded her of Michael. He had also claimed to be a convert. Lela tried to push Michael to the back of her mind and decided to give Jake a break. She felt some empathy for his situation, so she backed off the comments and offered him a beverage, to which he declined. Jake stood and stretched, straightening his back before walking over to the porch rail to wait for Lela to speak again.

"I want us to be friends again but I don't know about anything more," she finally admitted.

"I think you're scared." He turned to her and gently urged her off her seat and nearer to him. "You do want more."

"Jake." She tried to stop him from advancing toward her but

he placed his fingers on her lips to silence her and wrapped his arms around her waist. It was a move he had made on her when they were younger. Whenever she had become annoyed with him, he would coax her back into his arms and she would eventually give in and forgive him. But that was then and this was now. She was no longer the dewy-eyed teenager he kept mistaking her for.

"I want friendship and love... marriage and a family." He spoke softly. "I want us to evolve more, slowly. We can take our time."

"Jake."

"I want all the good and all of the bad... and maybe after a while, you will want the same. A lifetime with you, if you're willing."

"Let go, Jake." Despite her squirming Jake held on to her waist as an overwhelming sense of panic shot through Lela all at once.

"Jake, let me go!"

She pushed him away and abruptly walked to the opposite end of the porch. Her reaction took him aback and he quickly realized he had triggered something. Unsure as to what to do, he stayed where he was and resisted the urge to go to her.

"When a woman tells you to stop you need to stop."

"Lela I didn't mean..."

"I don't care about what you meant... I need you to leave."

Jake watched as a look of panic took over Lela's features, and she began to cough and wheeze. She choked on her tears. Her eyes swelled and became puffy as she gasped for air. Lela felt dizzy; her knees buckled beneath her. Jake ignored her plea to leave and rushed to her side to catch her by her waist and lift her up into his arms. Even in her weakened state she attempted to resist his touch.

"Let me help you," he pleaded with a whisper. "Let me help."

Saved for a Season

# Chapter Eight
## Sisters

Tristan!" Patience's voice sounded demanding.

"Yes ma'am, I'm coming."

Tristan had left her husband's side, though he was obviously in a heightened state of agitation, and was on her way to the kitchen when she paused in the hallway to take a breath. Before she entered to find Patience busy coating chicken with flour to fry for the dinner.

"I thought you had lost your hearing for a second, girl," Patience remarked as Tristan leaned against the door frame.

"Sorry, momma. I was talking to *my husband* like you suggested."

"Uh huh, well get to chopping those onions and bell peppers for the dressing."

"Onions."

"What's the problem?"

"No problem, momma."

Tristan retrieved a knife from the drawer and commenced with the chore she hated, trying to keep the fragrance from hitting her eyes as long as she could.

"So tell me about the doctor's appointment. What did she say?"

"Nothing yet, but I am sure everything is fine. It was just a routine check-up."

"You didn't sound that way earlier today."

"Well, you were pestering me."

"I didn't know showing concern was pestering."

"I keep telling you, I'm fine." Patience was distraught. "Now let it go."

"Hello, hello, hello..." a bellow came from the front door. "Where are you guys?"

An uneasy feeling swept through Tristan and landed in the pit of her stomach. She glanced over to her mother with a look of disapproval.

"I can't believe you invited her," Tristan whispered.

"If I didn't invite your sister I would have never heard the end of it." Patience was glad that the attention was off her.

"You know we don't get along." Tristan could barely stand to be in the same room with Camille.

"That's unfortunate."

Though her given name was Camille, in Tristan's opinion, her real name should be, Liar. Their mother, Patience, had named her daughter Camille Esther, after a woman of God's choosing, but Tristan still thought her real name was liar.

She was, what many called, an anointed woman; blessings seem to just fall in her lap. But Tristan knew better. Camille traveled the world with her husband, Leland, and had achieved much success. Camille had a real gift for making money and made more than her fair share; all on a lie. It had only taken one lie. One: The only one she refused to repent for, despite the inevitable outcome. Tristan wasn't the jealous type but it angered her to watch how her sister gained success. Tristan was bitter and broken; and she knew the truth or at least she thought she knew the truth: That Camille had stolen Tristan's blessing. She had seized an opportunity that Tristan had ignored, even though Camille always argued that Tristan gave up and therefore, she got what she deserved.

Camille was the epitome of perfection. She had a wonderful husband, a brilliant child and the picture perfect life -- at least that seemed to be the case to everyone else.

When they were younger, Camille had preferred to be called Cami. Camille had been eccentric, with a flair for the dramatic -- so much so that she had chosen to get married right out of high school, and to Leland --Tristan's true first love. Why he'd chosen Camille over Tristan, she never understood and it used to burn her every time she had to face him.

After struggling for a few years, Leland started his own business and soon he was landing big contracts with influential people who helped him break into the commercial real estate market. Cami very quickly became Camille again as she said they had an image to uphold sounding very much like her mother. Leland traveled so much that whatever Camille wanted she got, and every now and then a gift would appear at Tristan's door, no name attached but she always knew who it was from. It was Leland's way of easing his guilt. Tristan never told anyone about the gifts, not even Lela.

The sisters were close when they were younger as there was only a year between their ages. And there was a time when Tristan tried to be truly happy for her sister's marriage and success but time had created a void in their relationship, not to mention all the jealousy.

Camille strutted into the brightly lit kitchen wearing stiletto heels and a size four two-piece suit. Camille strategically placed her high-end purse on the counter so that the designer label would be face up and in full view for everyone.

"Hello, momma." She moved right past Tristan to give Patience a hug.

"Hi, child I'm glad you're here so you can help."

"Help?"

"Yes, help. H-E-L-P," Patience retorted while pointing to the cabinets. "Reach in there and grab a big bowl, then grab those pans of corn bread over there to *help* your sister with the dressing."

"Yes, ma'am." Camille pouted, looking down at her freshly manicured nails, but she knew better than to question any further. Without speaking to her sister, Camille began mixing the ingredients together. After a few moments of silence, Camille decided to recognize Tristan's presence and looked up at her from across the kitchen table.

"I saw Jeff yesterday."

Camille was prying, but Tristan remained silent. Camille cleared her throat.

"He was at Mr. Wilken's shop."

Tristan remained silent.

"So, Leland and I went over to speak." Camille looked for some type of reaction from her sister, but found none. "Well, it seems that Jeff was looking for a job and he asked Mr. Wilken to hire him."

"Hello, to you, too, Cami... and how are you today?" Tristan asked with sarcasm.

"Oh, stop being funny and tell us about Jeff. I think it's good that he is trying to get work instead of hanging out all the time like a bum."

"I'm surprised you care. None of this has anything to do with you?" Tristan looked up at her sister.

"I am not as self absorbed as you would like to think I am. Besides, I know that the two of you have been having money problems and I just wanted to encourage you."

Patience listened to her girls go back and forth and resisted the urge to interfere.

"We are not having money problems and if we were it would be none of your business."

"Anyway," Camille sighed, "Mr. Wilken hired him as a full-time mechanic."

Tristan's eyes remained on her task.

"Thank you for informing me of something I already know."

"You know, Tristan, if the two of you were having money problems all you had to do was ask me for help. I could have hired Jeff, you know; maybe as Leland's personal assistant or something." Camille's voice was thick with arrogance.

At that moment, Tristan remembered playing in her grandmother's front yard, making mini sand castles and mud pies out of sand and water. Her sister would see that her sand castles were neater than hers and in a fit would stamp Tristan's castle down with her tiny feet. A steaming mad Tristan would then turn and run to her grandmother.

"Ma!" she would scream, and Ma would come out the

house, switch in hand. She wouldn't punish Camille, but instead, chastise Tristan.

"Stop complaining. Don't you see, she's just unable to do what you do, so she takes her anger out on you."

Ma would kneel down next to Tristan.

"It's Camille's life, and she will ruin it with those tantrums of hers. But don't get angry, Tristan, feel sorry for her instead."

"I don't want to feel sorry for her!" She would pout. "I want my sand castle back."

"Don't worry, Tristan, you'll get it back in time." Tristan remembered looking at Ma with curiosity. She had no earthly idea what she was talking about. In time, what did time have to do with her sand castle? As if Ma were reading her mind, she answered.

"Destiny is a crazy trip down life, and when you disregard your own truth for the path of others, you're playing a game with destiny; and that's dangerous."

"Yes, Ma?" Tristan had answered, as confused as ever at the age of eight.

"You'll find out." Ma paused and looked up at the sky, then slowly raised her body; cursing under her breath. "You keep letting Camille take what's yours and in time, you'll figure it out. But be warned, if you start to play games with others lives, you will reap what you sow."

Tristan hadn't figured it out. It was now twenty years later and, she was still crying over crushed sand castles.

"Look, Camille, you have no power over who Leland hires or fires, so stop acting like you do. Because you and I both know Leland already offered Jeff a job, and he didn't want it. So, thanks but no thanks, Camille. Your help is not wanted."

"So, you went to Leland behind my back?" Camille rolled her eyes. "How sneaky of you. What else have you and *my* husband been discussing?"

"Well, first of all, what I discuss with *my* clients is confidential and what I discuss with *my* friends is none of your business. If you have a communication problem with your husband, maybe you should take that up with him."

"What!" Camille sputtered, but Patience had had enough.

"Okay girls, enough talking and more cooking." All she needed was another reason for her daughters to hate each other. "Camille, set the table for thirteen."

"No, wait! I want to know what's she is talking about."

"No! Who you telling no? Huh…" Patience held up a wooden spoon and was waving it from side to side. "Now   go set the damn table."

"Fine, who's coming?" Camille sulked.

"Does it matter? I asked you to do something, do it."

A small smirk came across Tristan's face as she relished in her sister's reaction to their mother's orders. Patience turned to Tristan with a concerned expression on her face.

"What's wrong, mama?" Tristan asked.

"Everything, but besides what I just witnessed I think you should know that your brother is coming tonight and that he will be bringing Tanya."

"That doesn't bother me one bit." Tristan lied and held her breath. The very idea that Tanya was going to be in her home after what her mother had claimed that very same afternoon was embarrassing, especially now that Camille and Leland were there.

# Chapter Nine
## Vulnerability

Lela watched helplessly as Jake removed the ice pack from her forehead. Still in a weakened state, she closed her eyes in the hopes that the dizziness would fade. Jake laid her on the sofa and sat by her side, consistently ordering her to breathe deeply and quietly. He waited on Lela, giving her water to drink, though it seemed that no matter how much she drank her mouth felt like it was full of cotton.

"Maybe you should get some sleep," Jake commented with concern.

"No, I'll be fine."

"I'm sorry if I scared you," he whispered gently.

"It's okay. I sort of over reacted." Jake observed that her breathing was regular and she had stopped sweating.

"Well, since you feel better, unless you need something else, I'll leave."

"No... don't go." Lela reached over and touched his shoulder. "I'm sorry. I guess I'm sending you all types of mixed messages."

"You have nothing to be sorry about but you really should rest."

Lela shut her eyes for a moment and gathered her words together, Lela wanted to tell Jake everything but her mind urged her not to trust him.

"I'm afraid, you know."

"Afraid of what Lela... Me?"

"No. Not you..." She paused, "Yes, you... but..."

The whistling of the phone cut into their conversation and caught her off guard, although Lela saw the interruption as a good way to avoid their future conversation.

"I should pick that up." Lela slowly sat up, still a bit flustered.

"Let it ring, you need to rest," Jake objected, but Lela ignored him and gathered her strength to get up from her sofa. She grabbed the phone.

"Hello."

"I want you to come over for dinner," Tristan commanded, sounding rushed.

"I can't, Tristan. Jake is here."

"Great … even better. He and Jeff can make up. So, I'll see you in a few?"

"Tristan… we're kind of in the middle of something."

"You two are always in the middle of something. Come over. My mother is here, and I told Jeff about the pregnancy but he was liquored up and moody. Besides, my sister and her family are here and I need a buffer."

Lela was insulted.

"No, thanks. I really don't feel like being your buffer."

"You're my best friend or at least you once were. Come on!"

Although she hated the idea of a dinner party Lela was exhausted from her conversation with Jake and didn't want to risk another episode. So, she saw the invitation as a way to smooth things over, at least for a while.

"We'll be there in about thirty minutes."

Jake listened to Lela's end of the conversation, and although he knew that Lela had a lot that she needed to get off her chest, he didn't want to push her into a corner. Lela put down the phone and turned to Jake, only to find him standing behind her.

"You shouldn't sneak up on people."

"I wasn't sneaking, but I'll announce my presence next time."

"Were you listening?"

"Yes."

"Do you mind going over to Tristan's for dinner?"

"Are you running away from me?"

"I can't be alone with you right now."

"I understand, although I don't know why." He rubbed the back of his neck, "So, I'll go."

"Great." She sighed. "Tristan mentioned that you and Jeff don't get along much anymore."

"We have our differences."

"I don't know what happened between you two but don't you think that now is the perfect time to work it out?" Lela watched him fold his arms in contemplation. "I mean you can't have that much animosity between you, you went to his wedding."

"I came to that wedding to see you."

"And I'm grateful you did, but you're a man of God now. You can't afford to hold on to grudges."

Jake knew she was right, but was uncomfortable with hanging around Jeff. Their lifestyles clashed when he got saved and it was hard for him to hold on to any of his old friendships. Jeff was no exception.

"If I were to share something with you, would you repeat it to Tristan?"

"We're kind of working on our friendship right now."

"Yes, I know. But as *your* friend and as someone I really care for, as someone who wants to be closer to you..." he paused. "Could I trust that what we talk about would not leave the two of us?" Jake fought the urge to try and hold her again and maintained his distance from her. "I meant it... I meant what I said... I want to be closer to you."

"I know you do." She answered quietly. "Let's go..."

Without any more conversation, Jake took her by the hand and led her outside to his car. He proceeded to open her door for her and then made his way to the driver side. Lela sank into his car seat and allowed her head to fall against the headrest. She felt relaxed for the first time that evening, so she decided to rest her eyes. Jake slipped on a gospel jazz track and watched Lela drift into a light sleep. The sound of smooth tunes filled the car. Just an hour after an anxiety attack, Lela felt secure and safe for the first time in months.

"What an oxymoron," she commented, coming out of her tired daze.

"What?"

"You managed to bring me happiness, confusion, anxiety and relaxation all in one evening. I don't know if that's a good thing or a bad thing."

"Well, I definitely don't want to be the cause of your anxiety or confusion." Jake kept his eyes on the road as they drove for a while. "So, can I confide in you?" he finally spoke.

"Sure, but I don't want you to be mislead."

"All I need to know is that I don't have to worry that what I say to you will travel to anyone, despite whatever happens between us."

"I promise that whatever we talk about will stay between us."

Jake knew that she didn't take her promises lightly.

"Jeff was cheating on Tristan, that's why we fell out."

He waited for Lela to reply. He tried to glance in her direction to see her expression but she remained silent.

"He was seeing, Tanya. I kept telling him he was wrong and that he should break it off before someone got hurt. That it wasn't right, but he didn't want to listen."

"Tanya..." Lela rolled her eyes, "Tanya Spencer?"

"The one and only"

"I thought she was dating Eugene."

"When did that happen?"

"A few months ago, according to Tristan. I wonder if he knows about...?" Her voice grew to a whisper.

"Who knows?"

"Eugene. According to Tristan, they've known each other for years, so... he may know." She answered herself. "Is Jeff still seeing Tanya?"

"I don't know," Jake said. "I hope not. Besides, we stopped speaking a long time ago. He called me a hypocrite. Said that I used to do that sort of thing all the time and he didn't believe that I was capable of changing." His voice cracked.

"You're capable Jake, you are." Lela smiled.

Jake needed to hear those words from her. Jake cleared his throat in an attempt to shift the topic.

"So, do you mind telling me about the anxiety attack? What happened?"

Lela bit her lower lip. She knew he would eventually want to know the origin of her attack but she wasn't ready to share that part of her history.

"I know you mean well, but I can't."

"Why won't you let me in?"

"Jake... It's not that I don't want to, I just can't right now."

Lela noticed him tighten his grip on the steering wheel. She knew he had to be frustrated. Lela looked out her window, the night sky was sparkling; she noticed light drops of rain hitting the glass at a snail's space, and then quickening. She turned back to Jake. He had turned on the windshield wipers and was silently moving his lips. Not wanting to cause any more uncomfortable moments, Lela kept her thoughts to herself and they rode in silence the rest of the way.

Saved for a Season

# Chapter Ten
### Family Dinner

"I don't want to eat them!" Camille's six-year-old son, Lee, was adamant about his dislike of beets and was not willing to yield on the matter. Sitting between his parents, Camille and Leland, he started to wail. The sound of his screeching was like nails driving into Tristan's skull.

"But they're good for you, honey." Camille was weakly trying to urge her son to eat.

"Leave him alone ... if he doesn't want to eat them, don't make him." Leland moved the plate from in front of his son, making Lee very happy. Camille sat back in her chair, miffed. She loathed how her husband undercut her authority. Camille watched her husband as he picked at his food and imagined him choking on a chicken bone.

"Don't tell me to leave him alone, the boy needs discipline."

"The boy needs to be left alone."

"The boy has a name," interjected Patience.

The dinner table was crowded with guests. Next to Camille was Mr. Wilken, a pleasant old man who refused to retire; to the dismay of his wife of forty years, Darla, who was busy serving her husband more potatoes. At the head of the table was Patience who watched as Camille struggled with her child.

"Beets are good for a growing boy. I know I love them and would hope my grandchild would try to eat them, just for me." At the request of his grandma, Lee reached for his plate and began eating.

"Jeff, are you enjoying your dinner?" Patience asked.

"Oh, yes, ma'am," Jeff spoke between bites.

"You can thank your wife for most of it."

"Thank you, baby." Their eyes met for a moment. Tristan was adjacent to her husband; her brother Eugene was to her left and next to him was Tanya, followed by the mouth of the south, Ms. Sutter.

"Yes, dear, thank you..." Ms. Sutter chimed in.

"I helped too." Camille refused to allow Tristan to take all the credit.

"Yes, yes, they both helped..." Patience remarked, "So, Jeff, I hear you will be working with Manny at the shop?"

"Uh, yeah... I start tomorrow." Jeff stole a glance at Tanya, it was apparent that she was uncomfortable. A knock came from the front door.

"I'll get it." Patience announced.

"Well, who else was supposed to be coming?" Jeff asked.

"Jake and Lela," Tristan answered. Jeff dropped his fork on his plate, causing a loud clang. Patience returned to the room, followed by Jake and Lela, who greeted everyone, then found their places at the table.

"So, Lela, you and Jake are back together?" Patience inquired.

"Mom, that sounds like personal information," Tristan cut in.

Jake looked over at Lela who had stuffed a piece of bread in her mouth, hoping no one would ask her questions. Seeing she was unable to answer, Jake shook his head in the negative.

"No, ma'am. We're just friends."

Jeff chuckled under his breath, letting his obvious distain for Jake go public,

"Smart choice, Lela." Jeff cut his eyes at Jake.

"What do you mean by that?" Lela inquired.

"You do know his past. Mr. Preacher man is no saint, no matter what lies he has told you."

Jake listened as Jeff poured scorn on his character. "All the prayers in the world won't get him forgiven."

"That's enough, Jeff," Tristan cut in.

"Don't tell me what's enough!" Jeff hissed. "He comes in my home waving his snotty self-righteous nose in my face and I'm supposed to just sit here and take it?"

"Jeff, what has gotten into you? He hasn't done any such thing," Tristan countered.

Tristan's face grew hot with embarrassment as she noticed Ms. Sutters had sat back in her chair, sucking in every word that was uttered. Her eyes were wide with expectation and they weaved back and forth from Jake to Jeff, watching for each person's reaction.

"What if I told your parishioners at that church of yours all your dirty secrets, huh Jake? Do you think they would love you so much?"

Jake backed his chair away from the table. His movement was so abrupt that Jeff stood in anticipation of a show of aggression. The sound of the clock clicking could be heard from the kitchen as the guests got eerily quiet.

"I didn't come here to get into an argument, so I'll leave."

"Yeah, that's right. Run like you always do," Jeff taunted.

Jake stood and faced Jeff, who was stationed on the other side of the oblong table. He felt his hands tighten into fists and his jaw clinched stiff.

Lela watched Jake struggle to keep his composure and took a hold of his hand. He felt her fingers interlock with his and managed to calm himself down.

"I'm sorry if I've offended you. I'll leave." Jake spoke calmly.

"Oh… ok. So you're not going to get into this with me…" Jeff's eyes were wild and haughty, as if he were looking around the table to find an ally. He finally landed on Lela. "You do know he was never faithful to you. Ever."

"You might not want to start using words you don't know the meaning of, Jeff." Lela couldn't help but come to Jake's rescue.

She was certain her words would lead to a bundle of speculation but she felt obligated to put an end to his rant and gambled that he wouldn't press her in front of Tristan.

Jeff sat down, deflated by her confidence and unsure as to what Lela knew.

She squeezed Jake's hand, signaling that they should leave, and moved swiftly toward the front door.

Tristan observed the symmetry between the two. "Stay," Tristan asked.

"Actually, I think it's best if we go," Jake answered, his back facing the dining table.

"Let the *righteous* man go," Jeff chimed in.

"I'll walk you out." Tristan stood to escort the two the rest of the way. Upon reaching the door when they found that it was raining more heavily, Jake indicated that he would get his car while Lela waited. As soon as he left the doorway Tristan started to interrogate Lela.

"What do you know?"

"Not much."

"Liar."

"No... lying would be telling you I know nothing."

"Tell me what you know."

"It's none of my business."

"Not your business. You jumped on my man's head in there and I want to know why," Tristan hissed.

"If you want to get on me for talking to him like that then do so but I'm not telling you anything." Lela shook her head in frustration. "Even if I wanted to tell you, I couldn't."

"Does it concern me?"

"It doesn't matter because I'm not going to start this."

"What about our friendship? You're supposed to protect my interests."

"No, not protect your interests. I'm supposed to be there when you need me for support. But I won't be berated by anyone, not your husband or you."

"How is not telling me supporting me?"

"Tristan, no one's relationship is any body's business but their own. You told me that once."

"Yeah, so what. That was then."

"So... what I talk about with Jake is none of your business."

"This is bull, Lela. You're choosing him over me again!"

"I'm choosing me over you for the first time ever. I'm sorry if I can't continue to be at your beck and call but you only want me around when it's convenient for you."

"You have no idea what a real friend is," Tristan said with disgust.

"I know that whatever is going in your marriage is your business. Now, if you need a shoulder to cry on or someone to confide in, I'll be there. If you have great news and want someone to celebrate with, I'll be there. But you will not use me to get dirt on your husband so that you can trap him. Those types of games are for children."

Upon hearing their last words Jake wrapped his arms around Lela's waist, pulled her away from the door and under his umbrella.

"Let's go."

Tristan stalked back to the dinner party where Patience had managed to change the subject and the mood of the dinner by serving dessert early.

"So, you plan on staying in town for a while then? Patience was in the middle of questioning her son, Eugene.

"Huh. Yeah, I hope to stay permanently." He swallowed his food. "I think it's time I settled down and started a family."

"So, is that your big news?" The guests all stared at Eugene. Tanya had a mischievous smirk on her face and her lips twisted.

"Well, actually… We're engaged and we've decided that the wedding is in a month," he said.

The silence in the room was deafening. Patience never expected those words to come out of her son's mouth. Ms. Sutter glanced over at Patience, documenting her discomfort.

"In a month, that's sort of fast?" Ms. Sutter asked.

"Yeah, but we've known each other for a long time…" Jeff swallowed hard and placed his cutlery beside his plate. Tanya's arrogant smirk soon turned to a nervous flinch.

"Well, congrats." Mr. Wilken raised his glass. "Here's to many years of happiness."

The rest of the dinner guests followed his lead and raised

their glasses in what seemed to be a failed attempt to bring everyone together.

"This is amazing," Tristan stated.

"I know, but we have more news." Eugene smiles widened. "I was offered a teaching job in town and I have decided to accept it."

"That's wonderful! Now you can pay me back all that money I lent you," Leland joked.

"Ha, ha bro." Eugene laughed then turned his attention to his mother. "Ma, are you okay?"

Patience stared Tanya down from across the table. She shifted forward in her seat and delicately tapped her fingertips on the dining table.

"Yes, baby. I'm so proud about the job. I just wasn't expecting to hear the other news..." Patience paused and drummed her fingers at a slower pace as each tap made Tanya more nervous. "Is Tanya pregnant?" Patience inquired.

"Oh, my," Ms. Sutter exclaimed with a glimmer of excitement.

"Not cool, Ma." Eugene sounded defensive.

"Well, marriage just seems like a rash decision..." Patience was poised. Her voice never rose. "A decision you wouldn't usually make unless something prompted you."

Tanya hated the fact that they were talking about her as if she wasn't in the room. Eugene got up from his chair and knelt by Tanya's side.

"She is a wonderful woman and I would have married her no matter what the circumstances." He hesitated, "But we are having a baby."

"It was really a shock and we weren't planning it," Tanya stated.

"How far along are you?" Jeff stammered, avoiding her eyes.

"Isn't it obvious ... six months." She cut her eyes away.

Jeff now realized why Tanya looked like she had gained weight and knew with all certainty that the child she was having had to be his.

"God is surely blessing you," Ms. Sutter exclaimed, happy to be a witness to a full week's worth of gossip.

"Yeah... He has," Eugene uttered softly, certain that his mother was already scheming on a plan to break them up. He wanted the attention off of Tanya. "I heard Tristan has some good news, too. So, tell us, sis."

"She's pregnant," Patience cut in before Tristan could answer.

"Oh, my goodness!" Ms. Sutter chuckled with delight. "Two grandbabies, well I'll be!"

"I hope you don't lose this one, Tristan," Tanya uttered with venom.

"Now, you wait a minute," Patience stood. "I've tolerated you for a long time but I never liked you and now you think because you're carrying my son's child that you can get away with speaking to everyone any kind of way. I don't think so."

"Ma!" Eugene was horrified.

"Eugene, I don't know what side of stupid you're sitting on, but I hope you know what you're doing. How do you even know if that baby is yours?"

"Okay, everyone let's just calm down," Camille said.

It was a valid question, and everyone knew it, but Eugene ignored his mother and her concern.

The dinner soon broke up after the explosion of emotions. Patience was obviously distraught by her son's decision to marry Tanya, but had no proof as to why he shouldn't. She immediately retreated to the guest bedroom without saying goodnight to anyone.

Tristan proceeded to clean the kitchen while Camille helped in the dining room. When finished, Camille entered the kitchen and placed the last table settings on the counter next to Tristan who was standing at the sink.

"Can you believe Eugene?" Camille retorted.

"Yes. This is what he does."

"Makes stupid choices?"

"No. Surprises people..." Tristan chuckled, "...and how do you know it's a mistake?"

"Oh come on…" Cami made a choking expression. "Tanya of all people? She has the worst reputation ever, just like mom said. It's one thing to be friends with her, we all conceded to that, but to marry her. *Please*."

"Who are you to judge someone's reputation? She works hard as a nurse and she is not a dumb girl." Tristan paused. "She has her own place, pays her own bills…"

"Just because she can take care of herself doesn't make her the best choice to marry. Her values are completely out of whack."

"And yours are perfect?"

"Oh, don't start… my life is fine."

"Who are you trying to fool? The only person you are fooling is yourself. You're just happy because you have someone else to look down on."

"*Fooling*. I am not trying to fool anyone. And you should know better than to throw stones."

"You just stood here and judged Tanya, and now you're pissy because I turned it around on you. How does it feel to have your life put in the spot light for what it really is… sad."

"Am I supposed to be offended by that? You must be blind, Tristan. That woman has always been after your husband and now that he's off the market she suddenly decides to marry our brother instead. She will do anything to stay near your man."

"Well, you would know something about that, like the old saying goes – 'it takes one to know one'."

"What?"

"Oh, don't act dazed."

Tristan turned away from her sister and sat down at the small wooden table that was in the center of her kitchen. Camille was torn between the anger she had against her sister for her close friendship with her husband and the love she wished they had between them. There was once a time when they loved each other and could talk, but that time seemed so long ago. Remorse crept up on her as she followed Tristan with her eyes.

"Maybe I'm mistaken but it just seems that Tanya is always

up to something," Camille finally stated, pushing out the silence.

"What makes you think she wants *my* husband?"

"I don't know. I just don't trust her."

"Don't make your trust issues my problem."

"I don't have trust issues."

"Oh, really." Tristan looked at her. "So you are ok with Leland and I being friends and that the fact that I see him a lot because of business doesn't bother you, because you trust him."

Camille flinched, her nerves were showing and so was vulnerability. "Ok. Ok... I admit I have a problem with it, but wouldn't you?"

"Oh, hell yeah." She was honest. "But I wouldn't make you bear the brunt of my distrust of my husband. I could say a lot of things that would hurt your feelings and you know I could, because he tells me too much, but the real truth is, I have never slept with your husband, and I never will. Period."

"Why not?"

"Because you are my sister, and despite how we treat each other, your family and I love you." Tristan paused. "A little bit anyway."

Camille let out a soft chuckle, amazed at her sister's admission.

"Well, I'll be..." she sighed. "I guess, deep down I know you would never do such a thing, but you were always the better of the two of us."

Tristan nodded her head at her sister's silent insight and unspoken understanding. What Tristan refused to do, was not beneath Camille's ability and they both knew it.

"Well, everyone has their vice..." Tristan stated.

"I was afraid I was going to be alone," Camille admitted. "That's why I took him. I knew you would find someone else. I thought you would just get over it, I mean we were still teenagers."

"I did get over him," Tristan answered her unasked question. "It was the betrayal by my sister that I didn't get over."

"I'm sorry." Camille had a tear in her eye. "If it makes you feel any better, more than likely we will be ending this marriage some time soon."

"That doesn't make me feel better."

Tristan stood up and walked over to her sister, then wrapped her arms around her.

"I know you really did care for him and he cared for you, too. So, hang in there. Try counseling or something."

Camille smiled weakly and wiped a tear from her eye.

"Yeah, we are on our third marriage counselor. Didn't he tell you?"

"No, well... I suggested counseling to him, he flat out rejected it."

"Yeah, well... that makes sense."

"So, what now?" Tristan, emotionally tired, sat back down.

"So now, I try to figure out what the hell I am going to do with my life."

"So will I." Tristan followed.

"You already know what you're going to do."

"I do?"

"Yep, you're going to have a baby, but first go to a salon and get your hair done, because it looks a hot mess." Camille laughed lightly.

"Funny."

Tristan chortled and then picked at some left over coconut cake that her mother left on the table. She put her pinky finger in the icing getting hold of a large chunk and let it sit in her mouth allowing the sweet cream to dissolve into her tongue. Cami watched as her sister sucked on her finger like a child pouting. She reached for a slice of cake.

"You want some?" She questioned.

"Sure."

"No more hateful arguments." Tristan looked her in the eyes. "I can't take it anymore."

"I know, kid, I'm sorry." Camille took a huge slice for herself.

"You should enjoy this time and eat for two... Believe me

it's the only time you eat like a pig and don't regret it."

"In that case, pass me the whipped cream."    Tristan laughed.

Saved for a Season

# Chapter Eleven
## Friend

Jake sat in silence, watching the rain fall on his car's windshield, each drop slowly creating a path of water only to be cut off by the window washers. He waited. She was quietly seated in the passenger seat, looking out her window at her home. Part of her wanted to run inside, take the rest of her magic pills and forget about this day, but the other part of her was yearning for closure, to tell him what she was so afraid of. But could she? Finally, after what seemed like time suspended into nothingness, Lela turned to Jake.

"If the weather permits, Thursday, do you want to have a picnic?" She felt silly, asking him out. Why couldn't it just be two friends having a day out together?

"Sure," he replied. "We'll make a day of it."

"A day?"

"Yeah," he laughed. "Two friends, hanging out, spending a day together. Maybe we'll do some shopping, take in a movie and at the end of the day..." His voice trailed, and so did his purified mind, going to places he had long put aside.

"How about we just start with a picnic." She smiled, "friend."

"I'll call you." He chuckled as he saw the doubtful look on her face. "For real this time."

# Chapter Twelve
### Tangled Web of Lies

It rained through the night. The sound of water gently tapped on the rooftop and windows. The rain was usually soothing for Tristan but this night Jeff tossed and turned. Unintelligible sounds crept from his mouth while he slept. Tristan could barely open her eyes when the alarm went off. She gave a quick look over at the clock and saw the red numbers indicated it was 4:30 in the morning.

She made it a habit to be at the office by 6:30 every morning. So it required her to get up extra early to take care of her personal tasks. She then reached over with her hand and fumbled around the nightstand, knocking over her reading glasses. Tired and fed up with herself, she quickly shut the blaring alarm off, wondering why she even considered getting up so early to pray.

"He doesn't listen anyway," she mumbled.

Despite her growing unfaithfulness something inside her urged her on; she looked over at Jeff who, despite his rough night, managed to sleep through the noise. His mouth was open and snores crept softly from his nasal passages. Though no longer tossing, his face looked stressed and there was obvious tension on his forehead. The previous night's events had taken an obvious toll on him.

Tristan slowly rolled out of bed and crept her way to her dresser, holding her Bible by the spine. Tristan's father had given her the bible when she graduated from high school. She had been passionate about the Lord then and attended every church function. It was at church where she met Jeff, as his father was a minister.

They were friends for a long time before they started dating. He supported her career choice to become an attorney and visited her while she was away at college. Jeff was never much for school but he had the ambition to learn a trade which led him to become a certified mechanic. His mother never approved of his choice of career and even Tristan's law school friends doubted their relationship would survive. Tristan never cared about titles and she had known Jeff too long to give up on their relationship, though they had been through some difficult times. They broke up occasionally but always found their way back to each other. She always knew that they were going to be with each other forever, what she didn't know was how long forever was going to be.

Jeff didn't always want to be in a committed relationship and his behavior made her doubt that he would ever want to settle down. He had other plans and wanted to date other women.

Tristan looked in the bathroom mirror, poking the fresh bags under her eyes. She washed her face and slid into her flip flops, then treaded down the hallway. As her feet grazed the carpet, she peaked in on her mother, noting that she was still asleep and then continued to the living room. She threw her curtains open to see if the conditions outside had changed and saw only that the clouds were low and heavy and the ground was still soaked with standing water. The blacktop street glistened. Tristan frowned not wanting to have to trudge through the wet waters to get to work, and even thought about calling in sick.

Realizing that her day was off to a bad start, she sat on the floor in front of her arm chair and flipped her bible open, first thumbing through the pages, then settling on some words she had previously highlighted.

"*Proverb 31:10*" she said out loud "*A wife of noble character who can find, she is worth far more than rubies. She brings her husband good, not harm, all the days of her life.*"

Tristan couldn't continue and tears began to well up in her

eyes. When she found out she was pregnant she had mixed emotions about how she should proceed and even contemplated an abortion. But her fear of Jeff and her mother's reproach --if they ever found out --had easily outweighed the fear of having a child. Although fear was a great motivator, she was not convinced that it was a mistake to attempt to have this child and the idea of bringing a child into a home with Jeff was weighing heavily on her heart.

Deep inside she felt that something wasn't right with Jeff and it was more than his drinking. Everyone's behavior seemed to confirm her worry at the dinner party. On top of that, her sister's comments were drifting around in her head. Camille had said she didn't mean her comments, even she wasn't that great of a liar. Tristan laid face down on floor and she wept. She was tired and could no longer bear to hold on to the baggage of her past anymore. Her faith was weak but she had to talk to someone about what she had done. She stared at her bible, she could hear her pastor's voice – *when nothing else can work and you have no one to talk to, try Jesus.* Tristan closed her eyes and took a deep breath.

*God, I know I've done some unforgivable things, but please forgive me. My marriage is falling apart at the seams. My lies have caused so much pain and I know I need to tell the truth but I don't know how. I'm afraid he'll leave me. Please forgive me and help my marriage. I was wrong but I just don't understand why things have to work out this way. I don't know my husband, I don't know this man and it just seems that I can't keep him happy. But I love him, Lord; I want my husband to love me.*

Tristan shuddered as a chill ran through her body, she really needed some answers. Not able to think, she rolled over on her back and stared at the ceiling. Tristan thought about how many things she had refrained from doing while in college. She didn't drink, smoke, try drugs, have sex, but that changed when Jeff came back into her life. She had been desperate and willing to do anything to keep him. She remembered the conversation she had with Jeff a few months after they decided to get back together. He begged her to go out of town with him for an overnight vacation, and against her better judgment she had agreed.

"Do you even think about sex?" Jeff had asked her.

"Of course, I do," she'd told him. She had been nervous. He had been bringing up this subject a lot. Tristan had pushed her hair behind her ear to reveal an uneven bright red mark on her neck, which Jeff had placed there moments before. "But I can't sleep with you. You understand, don't you?"

"I used to understand but we're not kids anymore. We don't live with our parents and no one is watching."

"I thought you believed the same things I do." Tristan watched as Jeff popped his knuckles.

"Look, I love you and I want to show you I love you."

"But you do, Jeff."

"No, Tristan, I want to show you in a more intimate way."

"We don't need to have sex to show each other that we love one another."

"Come on, Tristan. We are adults and I need to know you love me."

"You don't think I love you?"

"Not as much as I love you."

"Jeff, that's not fair."

"If you can't give me what I need I can't be with you. And what I need is for you to show me how much you really love me."

It had been all lies but at the time she had felt so desperate to keep him, she gave in. Now, years later, she felt just as desperate. Now, she was the one keeping secrets and telling lies and felt like she was being punished, but if Jeff ever knew the truth she would surely lose him.

Her thoughts began to wander to the words of her grandmother, 'You'll reap what you sow,' and then to the email she received from Tanya. Tristan temporarily shrugged off her curiosity and decided not to indulge in her pity party any longer than she needed, but soon she found she was unwilling to let sleeping dogs lie. Without thinking on it any further, she went to her office and looked up the email from Tanya that she still had not read.

Her eyes skimmed the first line, then slowed abruptly. Tristan could barely believe what she was reading.

*I think you should know...* she read *...I'm carrying your husband's child...* Tristan's mouth dropped as she read on. *...I know you won't believe me, but I never meant for this to happen. I just want him to accept responsibility. I wanted to tell you sooner but I was scared and he threatened to tell Eugene...* This has got to be a joke, Tristan thought; *...I know this is a surprise but I couldn't think of a better way to tell you. Just so you know, Eugene is already aware and he has asked me to marry him.* Tristan sat back with tears in her eyes. How could he? she thought. How could my brother marry a woman who'd had an affair with his sister's husband? How could Jeff sleep with Tanya! Tristan was sickened and felt her stomach churn from anxiety and before she could reach the bathroom, she hurled what was left of her late night dinner on the hall carpet. She felt too ill to try to reach the bathroom so she decided to stay where she was, crying.

Saved for a Season

# Chapter Thirteen
## The Beginning of the End

When the sun finally showed its face again, it dried up the remaining water which gave Lela and Jake a perfect opportunity to make good on their picnic date.

*Date*? Jake was still wondering if he had messed up with Lela in the car by stating that it was two *friends* spending the day with each other, but Lela seemed unfazed in her blue denim pants and white cotton blouse, adorned with deep purple and yellow flowers. To him, she was absolutely beautiful, and he could not remember a time he'd felt so encouraged to see a woman's face. They were able to find a spot that was clear of people and planted themselves upon a dark green blanket with a basket filled with finger foods prepared by Lela.

A large magnolia tree shaded them from the brilliant sun as they sipped their freshly squeezed lemonade in silence. Jake watched Lela. He liked to watch her, paying attention to her mannerisms. She still bit her inner cheek when thinking and twisted her lips when concentrating, but now she didn't move around as much. He also noticed that she kept a small bottle of pills in her handbag, which she clutched tightly. Also, something else that Jake noticed, which concerned him even more than the pills, was her inability to fully relax. When greeted by strangers Lela tensed up and when Jake offered his hand to her as she sat down on the blanket, she immediately resisted, insisting she could handle it herself. It was confusing for Jake and he wished he knew what it was that kept her at arm's length.

"Enjoying your cheese?" Lela noticed his stares and wished he would stop.

"Yes, I have never had this kind before. It's different."

"It is best with red wine, but I figured you didn't drink anymore."

"You would be right," Jake nodded. "I didn't know you drank." It was as much a statement as a question, to which Lela just smiled.

"There's a lot you don't know about me, Jake."

"Care to share?" His tone was almost pleading but he didn't want to push it.

"No. Not really. Not yet." She spoke in almost a whisper, as if letting the thought float out.

"Hey!" A shout came from the other side of the park. Lela and Jake turned to see if they could find out where the yell had originated. "Help me!" a female voice hollered again. With that, Jake was on his feet and running toward what look like a couple in the midst of a very heated argument. Lela could feel her heart racing and her head exploding from pain.

"No!" She screamed at Jake. "Don't leave me!"

What was she doing? There was a woman that needed help and Lela was only thinking of herself. But she couldn't breathe. Oh God she couldn't breathe. She watched as Jake confronted a man as he was about to strike his female companion, only to be struck himself. Lela couldn't believe her eyes and she couldn't just stand there, either. So, she ran toward them, screaming.

"I called the police, I called the police and they are coming!" The man and woman both became startled and ran out of the park toward the street, leaving Jake confused.

"Oh my," Lela gasped as she touched the bruise that was now forming under his eye.

"He hit me, can you believe that?"

"Well, yeah." Lela cocked her head to the side. "Let's get you some ice for that."

"I don't need ice."

"Yes, you do!"

"Okay." Jake gave in. "So where are the police?"

"Oh, I lied. Sorry. I was just trying to scare him away."

"Yeah, I hate to say it, but there is a time for everything."

"This from a preacher." Lela laughed.


Camille sat in the mall parking lot and checked her shopping list. Leland had texted her with a new request for items he needed within the hour for an important meeting. After she had finally gathered everything she needed and was about to go meet him, she became distracted, watching an elderly woman struggle to make it into the mall. The woman looked fragile and it seemed that she was in a hurry. Suddenly, to Camille's horror the woman stopped in her tracks and began to cry uncontrollably. As she watched, Camille became aware that the woman had soiled herself, and seemed to be in complete disarray.

*Oh, how horrible*, she thought. Camille grabbed her purse, jumped out of the car and ran to the woman.

"Don't worry," she whispered in her ear. "Come with me." She led the woman inside the mall and to the department store bathroom.

"Stay here," she instructed the woman. "I will be right back."

Not in any position to refuse, the woman entered a bathroom stall and waited on Camille's return. It took Camille twenty minutes to find all she needed and return to the bathroom. Camille said nothing as she handed the woman a wash cloth, some baby wipes, a change of clothes and an extra bag.

"Thank you," the woman said quietly.

Camille waited for the woman to come out of the stall in order to check her size. She had guessed right, as she assumed she was the same size as her mother. Satisfied, she handed the woman the receipts for the purchases and left the mall.

When she returned to the car, she found a new text from Leland: *WHERE THE HELL ARE YOU? YOU'RE LATE!*

"No, he didn't!" Camille vexed and pressed Leland's number.

"Where are you?" he screamed

"How about asking me, if I'm okay."

"Are you hurt?"

"No."

"Then what the hell are you talking about? I needed you here ten minutes ago, and you said you would be here!"

"Look, I'm sorry. I ran into a bit of an emergency … I had to help someone."

"Who?"

"A woman you don't know."

"Do you know her?"

"No, I had never seen her before, but she really needed help, so I helped her."

"No! You did this crap on purpose. You knew I needed those items for the deal and you sat on your fat ass on purpose. Just to spite me!"

"Are you kidding me?" Camille couldn't believe her ears. "Why are you talking to me this way?"

"Because I'm sick of you," he spat.

"Well, that makes two of us," she hissed. "You're a jackass, Leland and I want a divorce!"

"What!"

"You heard me. You can't even take the time to find out why I'm late and you assume that I would hurt your businesses on purpose. The same businesses I helped build with you, the same businesses that put food on our table. Well, if you think I am that horrible, we don't need to be together. I don't want to be with someone who would rather treat me like their secretary than their wife!" She screamed, "And don't think I won't take you for all that you're worth, you pig-headed prick!"

With that, she slammed her phone closed and punched in the number for Tristan.

# Chapter Fourteen
## Family over Business

Tristan picked up her cell phone and stared out her office window. Leland had called her three times within the hour and she had ignored every call. She already knew why he was calling because Camille had already filled her in. Yet, his persistence was getting on her nerves and it finally wore her down.

"Why haven't you called me back?" Leland bellowed through her earpiece, sending waves of static through her ear drums.

"I apologize, Leland, but I do have other clients and a full schedule of work. Now, is there a problem with the deal?"

"Problem with the deal? No, that's fine. My problem is my wife. She wants a divorce and is threatening to take half my earnings!" He was livid. "I want you to stop her!"

Tristan rolled her eyes, then cleared her throat.

"Look Leland, I cannot help you with that. I am not a family law attorney."

"But you're my attorney!"

"Not for a divorce. You'll have to find someone else for that."

"No way. I want you. I'll pay you whatever you want, just get this done for me. Besides you have all the dirt on your sister that I need to get what I want."

"I will not do that. Besides it would be a conflict of interest." Tristan was enraged at the idea that she could be bought to help him railroad her sister, but controlled her tongue.

"You can't do it, or you won't."

"Both. Leland, I will not represent you for your divorce. You will have to find another attorney for that, and if that upsets you, I apologize and will understand if you decide to also find another attorney for your other business dealings."

"What, What!" Leland stammered, "I don't want another attorney. You're the best ... I've known you forever and you know how I work."

"Well."

"Okay... Fine. Can you a least give me a recommendation?"

"No."

"Why not?"

"Because if the outcome is not what you want, you'll blame me."

"I won't."

"You will."

"Fine." Leland gave up. "Do you have any advice for me?"

"As a friend, I can tell you that you are more than screwed. You married in Florida, you live in Florida and your business is based in Florida. You married without a pre-nuptial agreement and have a kid, which your wife takes care of. She also helped you start your business and backed many of your real estate investments with her own money..." Tristan sighed. "So the best advice I can give you, is to stock up on some pens for all those checks you're going to be writing."

Tristan could hear Leland sobbing on the other end.

"Okay, Leland. I have to go, now."

Leland was still sobbing when she closed her cell phone. She felt for her friend and her sister but also knew that whatever Camille got from the divorce, she certainly deserved for time served. Tristan just hoped that their fate wasn't an indicator of what was to come for her and Jeff.

# Chapter Fifteen
## Bad News

Lela sat calmly on her front porch, rocking in her chair and sipping honey-lemon tea. She watched as the morning fog faded and revealed a steady drizzle of rain. The weather had warmed a little but the water would not let up. She turned her attention away from the weather conditions and placed it back on her book. She looked over her notes and listened to her fax machine buzzing in her office. She expected that more ideas to modify her manuscript had come and she was awaiting Joyce's call regarding content changes.

The two had managed to come to a consensus a few weeks earlier about the inclusion of spiritual references, but all the changes were not completely ironed out. Lela had refused to back down on the issue; however she was willing to deal when Joyce assured her that the integrity of her book would not be lost. Tired of going back and forth Lela agreed and was now stuck doing more research and was beginning to lose her focus. Doubts crept into her spirit constantly but were quickly put to rest by her supporters, mainly her parents.

Upon hearing the fax stop, she hurried inside to see what Joyce had sent. From the entrance to her office, Lela could see the thin pen lines drawn all over her paper. If it wasn't for her love of writing, she might have screamed. But there would be no advancement without hard work, she knew.

She returned to her station on the porch; documents, cell and house phone in tow. Settled in, she waited... and Joyce didn't take long to call. Lela grabbed the phone and braced herself for what she feared might be a rocky conversation.

"Hello, Joyce."

"Hello, Lela." Jake's southern accent was unmistakable.

"Jake. Good morning. I was expecting someone else."

"Obviously."

"How are you?"

Lela had been worried about him since last night. He had not talked   much on the ride home or when he dropped her off and was clearly upset about the altercation even though he assured her he wasn't. Jake was more concerned about her reaction. She wasn't actually certain that Jake had heard her cry out not to leave her.

"I'm good. You sound chipper this morning. You must be on your porch?"

"I am," she sighed, "but I think I'm chipper because you called."

"Aw. You better watch it, Lela. I think you're flirting," he said with a chuckle.

"You caught me." Lela bit the inside of her cheek.

"Are you free for breakfast? My treat."

"Oh, I would love to, but I have some work I need to finish today and I can't put it off."

"Not even for me?"

"I certainly wish I could but my editor is going to call at any moment. I can't miss her."

"Um, that book is already coming between us," Jake joked as he listened as Lela laughed.

"Never."

"Well, are you free for lunch or dinner?"

She was flattered by his persistence but it simultaneously created an uneasy feeling in her.

"How about I call you when I am free."

Jake felt she was trying to dodge his invitation.

"Don't call me; I'll call you, huh?"

"Don't take it like that. I'm just really busy." Lela looked down at her notes, at a hand written note from Joyce that said: *How about something on getting over your fears???* Lela dropped the documents on the table next to her rocking chair. She knew she wasn't as busy as she put on, she was avoiding.

"Lela, if you don't want to hang out with me just say so. We can just be friends. But don't leave me hanging out here." His voice was a bit defensive.

"You know you're probably right." Lela wanted to be truthful.

"What? Wait." Jake hadn't been expecting that response.

"No. Jake you are right. I flirt with you one moment and push you away the next, and that's not fair to you. So, it would be better if we were just friends."

"Lela, I didn't mean."

"Well, if you didn't mean it, you shouldn't have brought it up. Anyway, it would be better this way. You don't want a woman that's broken anyway."

"Broken? What are you talking about?"

"I can't talk about this now."

"Well it sounds like you need to." Jake paused. "Why did you not want me to leave you yesterday?"

"What?" she acted like she didn't understand his question.

"Yesterday, at the park. When I went to help that lady, you yelled for me to come back, and not to leave you."

"You heard me?"

"Yes. What was that about?"

"I just didn't trust that situation … it seemed wrong, and I didn't want you to get hurt."

"Okay." He seemed satisfied with that answer. "Now tell me what's up with those pills you keep taking?"

"What? What pills?"

"Lela, don't act dumb. The blue pills you keep in your purse. I swear you pop them like candy."

"I do not!"

"You don't? Could have fooled me."

"How dare you! You don't know what I go through, you don't know me as well as you think you do, Jake."

"Okay, but I want to. That's what I am saying. I want to know you but you keep me at arm's length."

"Maybe that's where you need to be."

"Are you serious? A second ago, you were happy I called and now I need to be out of your life." He was frustrated.

"I cannot help what I feel and besides, you have no right to question me about my personal business."

"I'm just trying to help."

"No, you're trying to be all up in my business."

"Okay, Okay. Let's just calm down."

"I am calm. You calm down."

She wasn't calm; she was anxious and wanted to put a stop to this conversation. She felt completely out of control. He just wanted to know too much. Why couldn't he be satisfied with what she told him? Why did he have to dig so much?

"I'm concerned about you. Are you on some type of medication?"

"It's none of your damn business!"

Lela's call waiting suddenly broke into the conversation.

"Look, that's my editor. I have to go, so don't bother calling me back."

Lela clicked over without saying goodbye.

"Hello."

"Oh, you don't sound so good. You hate my notes." Joyce was driving from her home to her office and the sound of rushing pavement was funneling through the phone causing her to drop in and out."

"I can barely hear you Joyce?"

"Wait a second hon." Joyce pulled out her ear piece and switched the signal with quick precision. "Can you hear me now?"

"Much better…"

"You hate my notes?"

"I haven't really gone over them but I'm sure that they won't be that bad." She could care less about those notes; Jake's words were still ringing in her head. *I care about you.* If he knew my secret, he would run for the hills, she knew. No man could deal with what had happened to her. She could barely deal with it herself.

"Well, of course they're not bad. The changes will be great … you just have to see things my way." Joyce's voice pierced through Lela's thoughts.

"Uh, huh."

"Okay, dear. Well is there something significant you would like to talk to me about?

"Ummmm, no," Lela answered, still consumed with thoughts of Jake.

"Are you sure you're okay, you seem a bit distracted?"

"No, I'm fine," she stammered. "My research, I wanted to talk about my research."

"Yes?"

"I'm losing focus and this book was not supposed to be this hard coming."

"Nothing worthwhile comes easy, Lela. You should put that in your book."

"I'll think about it…" Lela dismissed her comment. "What I really need is some help."

*I need Jake's help*, she screamed inwardly. *Oh goodness, I want him to be a part of my life, but he would never understand. I need my pills.*

"Done. Do you need someone with you?"

"What?" Lela remembered their conversation. "No please don't send anyone here … that's last thing I want. I'll email you the details and someone can work on it from there."

"No, now I'm putting my foot down."

"Oh, goodness."

"I'll send help. Someone talented with great instincts that can help you out and I'll find them immediately."

"No, really…" Lela protested but Joyce wouldn't let it go, so Lela finally gave in. "Ok, fine."

"Fabulous, you see what we can accomplish when you talk to me Lela? "

Joyce arrived at her office but remained in her car in the parking garage, talking to Lela. "You are a very good writer but you need to relax and do what you do best. I must run, call me if you need me."

Lela hung up but felt a complete lack of confidence. The moment she had left her home to go to Tristan's wedding her life had become one crisis after another. She had stepped out of her home and right into a battle with herself.

*I do not have a drug problem,* she persisted. *And who does he think he is anyway, lecturing me?*

Lela cared about Jake but was unsure about what she really wanted. *I don't need a man in my life; I've done just as well without one.* She wanted that to be true, and in a way it was. She had a career and a home, but beyond that, her life felt incomplete. Lela didn't know whether to feel upset or triumphal. *Oh God, help me,* she prayed inwardly. *I don't know what to do.*

After several hours of working on her manuscript Lela put her pen and paper to the side and moved inside to her kitchen. Her thoughts had been on Jake for the better part of the day and she began to feel awful about how she had treated him. She didn't want to push him away but it was safer for her heart not to get involved.

Lela's cell phone vibrated. She glanced at the caller ID, and to her surprise the area code was out of state. She didn't recognize it, so she answered cautiously.

"Lela? Niwe Lela?" a female voice with a muddled accent spoke.

"Who is this?" Lela asked. She recognized the accent as Bemba. She knew the language because she had learned it from her college roommate, Kasuba. However, she was unsure about the voice on the other end of the line.

"It's *me.* Kasuba."

The southern African accent now became recognizable to Lela. Kasuba was one of Lela's rare friends in Colorado who was great at emails but tended to only call when she had extraordinary news.

"Where are you now?" Lela asked. "France, Brazil...?"

Kasuba was a global traveler. She was born an American, but had been adopted and raised by Zambians who immigrated to America and eventually became citizens.

"Unfortunately, it's not that exciting. I'm in Colorado,

visiting a few friends from school, but I'll be returning to Zambia in a few weeks to join my parents. But that's not why I'm calling." Lela heard tension in her friend's voice.

"What's wrong?"

"I needed to check up on you, since I heard the news. I wanted to make sure you were okay."

"Why wouldn't I be okay? What news?"

"Oh goodness, you don't know." Kasuba sounded furious. "I cannot believe they didn't call you!"

Lela began to breathe heavily, but tried to remain calm although her friend's reaction was scaring her.

"What is this about? Kasuba tell me."

"It's Michael."

His name rang in Lela's head as she braced herself for what Kasuba had to say. Kasuba managed to steady her voice, as much as she could, but the tension was still there.

"Lela," she paused, "Michael was released last week."

"What?"

"I'm sorry to tell you like this. The prison should have notified you."

"Released from prison?" Lela couldn't believe what she was hearing. "Are you sure?"

Lela knew very well that Kasuba was certain; she wouldn't dare call without knowing for a fact that Michael had been released. Kasuba had been there with her through the trial and when he was convicted.

"Wait a minute. He got fifteen years! Who in the hell let him out?"

"Apparently, the parole board had a hearing a few months ago. I found out by reading the newspaper that he had been released. But I wanted to make sure, so I called the police, the prison and the D.A." She sighed, "It's true."

"Why didn't any one call me?" Lela felt her throat tighten and a sharp pain shot through her chest. "How could they just let him go and not tell me? I had a right to be there! I had a right to testify"

Kasuba couldn't say a word, but tried to offer her

condolences. She knew the torment that Michael had put Lela through.

"You can file an appeal," she offered in advice. "File a restraining order, immediately."

"What if he shows up here?" Lela whispered, no longer listening to her friend. "Do you think he could find me?"

"He's on probation, Lela. He can't leave the county and he must register as a sexual predator."

"You think some registration is going to keep him from acting on all the threats he made over the years? You've got to be kidding me."

"Lela, I know it's scary." Kasuba tried to calm Lela's fears. "But they would not have released him if they thought he was going to be a threat. Besides he has to report to a parole officer. He's not going anywhere."

"Yeah, they told me that when he was convicted and now he's out on parole. For all I know he could be here."

Kasuba was silent; she didn't know what to say.

"Kasuba," Lela said softly.

"Yeah."

"Thanks for letting me know."

"I'm sorry I had to be the one, hon."

"You said you're going over to Zambia in a few weeks?

"Yeah."

"Take me with you." Lela laughed half-heartedly, as tears began to stream down her cheek.

"Anytime, Hon. You're welcome to join me, anytime." Kasuba was serious and Lela knew it, but she couldn't run anymore, she'd be running forever if she did.

"Tell me about the trip." Lela inquired.

She hoped that the change in subject would help clear her head of negative thoughts. Kasuba understood and without hesitation dove right into her story.

"Well, it's no big deal, but I'm going back to Zambia to work for an advertising company. "

"What? You pulling a nine to five, I don't think so. What the real reason you're going back?"

"I am also going to be helping start a small school in the Eastern Province. I'm trying to better myself."

"Sounds like an adventure. Will Dabwitso be there?"

Dabwitso was Kasuba's on again, off again, boyfriend since they were very young growing up in Kitwe.

"I don't know, and don't care."

Lela was surprised by Kasuba's answer.

"You two must be off again."

"How did you guess?"

"Well, what was it this time?"

Lela allowed Kasuba to ramble on about her endless love for a man who was always giving her an endless headache. No matter how dramatic Kasuba made her love story sound, Lela's thoughts remained on Michael. She wanted to call Jake and ask him to come over, but hated to admit that she felt safer when he was around.

"*Ukutangila tekufika.*"

Lela's thoughts were again interrupted by Kasuba speaking Bemba.

"You have to warn me before you switch languages Kasuba, what did you say."

"Sorry, I was saying that having a head start doesn't mean you'll arrive first. That is what I told him."

"Who?" Lela was confused.

"Dabwitso." Kasuba answered. "You're not listening, but I completely understand."

"I'm sorry. I'm just shocked by the news about Michael." She didn't want to say his name, but it was unavoidable.

"It's okay, really. I should let you go. You'll probably want to make some phone calls."

They finally ended the phone call. Lela wished her friend safe travels; then put the phone down pensively and as she felt weakened. Her whole world seemed to cave in on her. She looked around her home and observed that her house alarm was disarmed, her front door was unlocked and some windows were cracked open. Frantic, she began to run around the house closing doors and windows, making sure they were secure.

Overwhelmed by anxiety, she collapsed into her sofa, feeling dizzy. She struggled to catch her breath; her eyes burned and tears streamed down her face. A heavy sense of terror consumed her. How could they let him go, she thought, how could they let him go? She started to search for her pocket book, she needed her pills. She felt like she would drown if she didn't get her hand on her pills.

# Chapter Sixteen
## Drowning

Lela arrived at her church an hour later, disoriented, her stomach grumbled from anger and lack of food. She entered the church office lobby. The church was expansive, a mixture of modern and aged architecture with huge lilac curtains draped over arched windows. Lela's tennis shoes squeaked as they came in contact with the waxed tiled floor. She would usually take the time to admire the environment but the reason for her visit was weighing heavily on her thoughts. The receptionist was not at her desk when Lela walked in but a buzzer rang when she opened the door to notify the attendant that someone had come in the facility. Soon after her entrance a short petite woman with gray hair stepped from behind a wall and glided over to the front desk, beaming with the brightest smile.

"Hi Lela. It's good to see you today. What brings you up here?" Ms. Brenda had been a member of the church from its inception and had gotten to know Lela since she first became a member.

"Hi Ms. Brenda. I called earlier and made an appointment to meet with Pastor Franklin." Lela was noticeably distraught and Brenda observed that her fists were clinched and her speech a little slurred.

"Oh, ok. I'll tell him you're here." She paused, then spoke.

"While you're here let me ask you, will you be holding your outreach meeting this week? I didn't see your name down on the room reservation list."

Lela huffed at the idea of having to do group this week. She wanted to be selfish but knew she couldn't -- others depended on her to be there.

"It should be Kate's turn this week. I didn't have the time to verify it but if not, let me know.'

"Let me double check while you're with the pastor and if not I will find a place for you somewhere."

"Thanks. I appreciate you letting me know."

Brenda nodded, then picked up her receiver and dialed the pastor's extension. After a brief conversation, she placed the receiver down and told Lela he was ready to see her. Lela walked down the corridor to the pastor's office. The closer she got, the more she wanted to run out the side exit. Lela was visibly frustrated, didn't want to talk with anyone about her problems, and didn't want to share her story any more. *It hurts like hell!* She screamed inside. *No one understands, no one! What am I doing here?*

As she came upon Pastor Franklin's office she observed that his door was wide open; she could see the pastor seated behind his desk. He seemed to be looking over some papers with his concordance open. As if he could hear her thoughts he marked the place in his book and stood up to greet her.

"It's good to see you, Lela. I'm glad you decided to come and talk. I haven't seen you in a while."

"Thanks for agreeing to see me at the last minute. I didn't know where else to go."

"By the sound of your voice this must be a personal matter?"

Lela hung her head, and felt her throat begin to tighten. Her eyes filled up with tears. She tried to keep her eyes from burning but to no avail. Pastor Franklin came from behind his desk, tissue in hand and led Lela to a seat.

"What's going on Lela?"

"I'm broken."

"Broken?"

"I'm afraid more during the day than not. I triple check the locks on my doors every time I leave the house or my car. I can't sleep at night and every time I hear a noise, I jump. I can't stand to be touched by a man and I cringe at the thought of being intimate. But, I'm incredibly lonely and the one guy that I ever had any true feelings for is being so kind to me, but I can't deal with it. I just want to push him away and he doesn't understand because he doesn't know…"

"Wait, slow down. Are you seeing someone?"

"No… that's just it, I can't. It terrifies me think about having to tell him what happened to me and why his touch can be so soothing at times but can give me the creeps at the same time. How do you tell a man that, without damaging his ego?"

"Let's stop and go back to the beginning. When you called me you sounded upset what sparked this?" Franklin brought a chair around and sat parallel to Lela and gave her his undivided attention.

"Michael is out of prison." Lela grabbed the tissue and wiped the tears away from her face. "They released him a week ago on parole. He could be anywhere by now."

Franklin sat forward in his chair and tried to decide how he was going to go about helping her. He could see the aggravation in her body language.

"You have every right to be angry and you have every right to be frustrated but I want you to remember the importance of the things we have talked about in group. Listen to my words Lela. Michael has no control over your life."

"I know that. Intellectually, it makes sense… but." She sniffed.

"You have worth, you are a child of the highest king and he will never leave you or forsake you. That man has no control over you."

"He raped me! He took my virginity. He took my pride. He took my security," Lela yelled. "He told me he was something he wasn't, he fed me lies and I ate every one of them. And I hate myself for it."

Pastor Franklin stayed quiet, allowing her words to be absorbed. He was not your average Pastor. Along with his many credentials he had a Ph.D. in psychology and a license to counsel. His passion for helping others came from his love of Christ and his own history. For he had been a victim of sexual abuse, a fact he had testified to on many occasions. After allowing Lela to calm down he spoke again.

"Don't let Michael win."

"He already won."

"You have a life to live. Don't be afraid to live it." Franklin looked in her eyes. "You are stronger than him."

"I don't feel strong," Lela stammered.

Franklin sat back in his chair and pondered his next words.

"What are you afraid of? I want you to verbalize what Michael being on parole has made you afraid of. Say it?"

Lela rolled her eyes; she didn't want to say it. She didn't want to think it, she wanted to go home and forget, hide.

"I'm afraid he'll violate his parole and come find me. That he'll do all those awful things again. I'm scared that I will never be able to move on because he breathes the same air as I do." Lela looked Pastor Franklin in the eye. "I hate him."

She paused, barely able to speak. "And the only thing I hate more than him, is what I have become because of him."

"What have you become?"

"Weak. I was never weak."

"You give him too much control."

"I gave him nothing, he took it."

"What he took was physical, but you are allowing him to take what is spiritual. He doesn't have that power, no man has that power."

"But he..."

"No buts, Lela! I will not let you give up. You are a survivor. That makes you stronger than he is or ever will be. But you have to believe it. I'll try not to tell you how you should progress or how you go about achieving that progression, but I will tell you this..." he paused to make sure Lela was fully listening. "Don't worry about this guy you obviously care about right now, concentrate on your personal self. You owe no explanation to anyone. If he is as great as he seems, he'll understand and he will wait until you are ready. Don't move any faster than you are willing to travel in your healing. It's your journey and nobody else's, including me."

"What if my friend doesn't want to see me ever again?"

"Then that's his loss and he doesn't deserve you. Lela, you should be proud of yourself."

"Why?"

"The fact that you are even contemplating the idea of getting into a relationship says you have come a long way. But that is not the goal, your spiritual happiness and well being is."

"Yes, I know."

Pastor stroked his chin in thoughtfulness. There was obviously something else on his mind. Lela waited quietly while he seemed to search for the proper words.

"Lela," he paused then looked her straight in the eyes. "Are you still seeing your therapist?"

"Sometimes, but not as often as before." Lela swallowed hard; she knew what his next question would be.

"Are you still taking medication?"

Lela felt a rush of fear come over her. *What a funny feeling*, she thought. What was she afraid of? No, this wasn't fear, it was shame. She was only supposed to take anti-anxiety medication for a limited time following her diagnosis four years ago, but she had kept asking for them and her doctor felt that she was doing the right thing so she continued to prescribe them. She also prescribed separate anti-depressants and even more pills to help her sleep. Lela didn't care for the anti-depression medication because she started to gain more weight, which she couldn't afford as she was already eating everything in front of her. She eventually stopped eating and started putting up barriers against people. She decided the best way to protect herself was to isolate herself. Occasionally, she took a sleeping pill when the anxiety pill didn't take the edge off and the nightmares got to be too much, but for the most part she was in too deep with the small blue pills. Even now as she sat in front of her Pastor, the sense of panic was intractable and grew as each moment passed. His eyes were watching her steadily and she felt them burn into her.

"Okay, I know I should stop taking them. I know I use them as a crutch, but..." She stammered, "I need them. I can't sleep without them and I still have nightmares!" She heard her voice rising to an uncontrollable level but didn't know how to ease her fury. She went from fearful, to shame, anger to rage. How dare he question her? She was the one who had been raped; she was the one who fought to get out of bed every day while she was in school. She was the one!

"You don't care. You don't know what I am going through. You sit here on your pedestal and judge the way I cope. I do what I can to keep moving and that's all I know how to do."

He wasn't talking, he was watching and listening.

"Why don't you say anything?" She was exhausted and her frustration began to show itself through tears that ran down her face.

Pastor Franklin wrapped his arms around her, like a trusted father. He held her while she cried, and he didn't let go and he didn't say a word.

# Chapter Seventeen
## Say What You Feel

Weeks had passed since Lela and Tristan had spoken to one another and Tristan began to miss her friend. On impulse she left work early and drove to Lela's home. Lela's car was parked on the side of her house but other than that there was no indication that anyone was home. Tristan crossed the driveway and noticed that Lela's front window was cracked open, an act that was out of the ordinary for Lela. Tristan then proceeded to knock on Lela's front door but there was no answer. Not one to give up she continued to knock.

"Lela," she yelled.

The silence gave Tristan an eerie feeling in the pit of her stomach. She watched as the porch swing moved eerily back and forth pushed by the breeze. The sight put fear in Tristan, who was unsure as to where Lela could be. She decided to search the porch for a spare house key. Lela was known for losing her keys or locking herself so she always had a spare key available. Remembering this Tristan continued to look. After a few moments she spotted a large flower pot filled with dirt but no plant. This seemed to be completely out of place and out of character for Lela so Tristan shuffled the flower pot over and discovered the spare key.

"Ha!" she belted, happy about her find. She proceeded to enter Lela's home. Tristan found Lela asleep on her sofa, completely oblivious to Tristan's intrusion. She glanced around the room to make sure no one else was there. Convinced she had over reacted she decided to leave but as she was about to walk out the door the house alarm went off. The blaring howl screeched continuously. Tristan covered her ears and ran over to Lela, who remarkably managed to stay asleep. She must be really tired, Tristan thought.

"Get up, girl!" Tristan yelled in Lela's ear. "Get up!" she pushed her. Lela jumped, heart racing and looked totally confused.

"What are you doing! Are you insane?" Lela ran over to her alarm box and disarmed it quickly, then shut the door that had been left ajar and locked it.

"How did you get in my house?" Lela asked enraged.

"I found your spare key under the flower pot. Why are you sleeping on the couch?"

"Give me my key."

"Oh, Lela… don't be mad."

"Now."

Tristan was shaken by her friend's forceful tone and immediately handed Lela the spare key.

"I guess I should thank you."

"For what?"

"Letting me see that my key was in the wrong place." Lela's heart was still beating fast she sat down to slow its pace.

"I'm sorry. I didn't realize I would scare you but I thought something was wrong."

"Tristan, you don't ever think of anyone but yourself."

"Harsh. I was totally thinking of you."

"You could have called."

Tristan stood pensive behind the sofa.

"I'm sorry, Lela. Truly I am."

"Why are you here? Why did you find it necessary to break into my house? Give me one reason I shouldn't throw you out."

"I know you're mad but I wanted to apologize. I missed you and wanted to talk to my friend. I realize how stupid I was being and I wanted to tell you. When I got here I saw your window up and when I knocked you didn't answer. I got worried."

"My window…" Lela looked confused; she didn't even

remember raising it. Not able to remember, she walked over and closed it. Her head ached from the scare and she was in no mood to argue so she decided to let it go. "Sit down Tristan, you're making me nervous."

Tristan immediately sat in the arm chair and watched as Lela took two pills from her purse and swallowed them without water before reclining once more on her sofa, eyes closed. The silence was deafening. All Tristan wanted was for Lela to say something.

As if Lela could sense Tristan's uneasiness she muttered, "I forgive you."

"Really?"

"Do I need to say it twice?"

"No... No..." Tristan fidgeted with her hands. "You were really knocked out when I came in, and the alarm didn't even wake you."

"I haven't been getting any sleep. I guess it caught up with me."

"I'm glad you're getting some rest." Tristan pickup a magazine that was in a rack near her chair and flipped through the pages.

"Is there anything else you need Tristan?"

"Have you heard about my brother and Tanya?"

"Yes."

"Who told you?"

"Ms. Sutter."

"That woman has a mouth as big as all out doors." Tristan placed the magazine back down.

"She called and left a message ... can you believe it?" They laughed. "Why aren't you at work?" Lela asked.

"I wanted to make sure we talked."

"So talk."

"I understand what you were talking about, you know about relationships." Tristan moved over to the sofa where Lela was now sitting up.

"And..."

"And... no one should be forced into doing something they

don't want to do. You didn't do anything to me and neither did Jake."

"Um."

"He's a good man. You two could be happy together." Tristan's statement was more of a question.

"We're not together."

"But you want to be, don't you?" Tristan noticed Lela's mouth get tight.

"I don't know."

"Sure you do. You two were practically in perfect sync the other night. You care for one another."

"I admit I care about him but we haven't spoken in a while. We had a disagreement."

"I'm sure it wasn't intentional. You know... when you start feeling new things for people and spending a lot of time together misunderstandings can happen." She paused. "So what was the misunderstanding about... was it about sex?"

As usual Tristan was off base.

"No, Tristan. Everything doesn't involve sex. Besides, Jake is not like that anymore."

"Ok. I was just going to say that you should be careful."

"Careful about what? The man is not pressuring me about anything. He is just trying to be my friend, which I wouldn't even let him do." Lela crossed her arms as if to guard her heart. "I tried to use the excuse that I was scared that he might try to take advantage of me. When the real problem is I was afraid of actually feeling something real for him and that he may be disappointed by me."

"Why would he be disappointed in you?"

"You wouldn't understand."

"Lela, I know I can be shallow and singled minded at times, but try me; I might surprise you."

Lela sighed, not knowing whether she could truly trust Tristan's olive branch but she desperately needed to talk about it, so she decided to dive in.

"Ok. Although intimacy isn't really an issue right now, one day he is going to want to get married, and with marriage comes intimacy…" She paused, "I'm afraid to trust, or to be intimate with a man. The thought of it scares me for many reasons."

"You mean," Tristan paused, and looked confused, "you don't want to have sex."

"I am human, Tristan. I have desires." Lela massaged her neck. "It's just that my fears outweigh my desires and whenever I feel urges in any way, they soon turn to disgust and I feel dirty."

"Why would you feel dirty?" Tristan was puzzled.

"Never mind. I've said too much as it is." Lela was about to give up.

"Lela, let me be your friend. Please share with me, don't push me away." Tristan pleaded.

Lela buried her head in her hands. She was drained and tired of keeping this secret.

"I was raped." She said it bluntly.

"Oh, my… Does Jake know?

"No." Lela shook her head, "and please don't tell him or anyone else."

"I won't." Tristan reached her arm around Lela to comfort her. "When did it happen?"

"My junior year in college. After Jake and I broke up, I met a guy. His name was Michael. He was the most sensitive, caring, generous man I had ever met." Lela bit her inside cheek. "I was a fool, in what I thought was love, but…"

"But what?"

"But I really didn't know him at all. And it was too late before I realized who he really was."

"He raped you?" Tristan was shocked.

Lela tucked her legs under her body and pulled herself inward like a cocoon.

"After six months of dating, he started asking me to marry him. And of course, I said no. At seven months he started to get weird, not so kind, not so understanding. So I told him, we need to take a break. He agreed and a couple of weeks went by without incident. Then he called, apologized for the attitude he was giving and told me he was just frustrated with classes and that he really loved me and wanted to be with me forever. Then he invited me to a frat party so that we could work things out."

"A party? You're not big on parties."

"Exactly. I had never been to a party my whole life, and the one time I decided to venture outside my comfort zone something bad happened."

"Well, why did you go?"

"He said he wanted to choose a public place where I wouldn't feel pressured and where I would be comfortable because people would be around."

"Were you drunk?"

"Would it matter?"

"No. I mean, it shouldn't." Tristan hesitated. "Well, did you tease him or something or lead him on?" Lela turned to see her eyes.

"Even if I did, which I did not, he had *no right* to touch me, or rape me. *No right.*" She said it firmly.

"I didn't mean to insinuate that it was your fault. I was just trying to get a better picture."

"Here's a picture for you... we met at the party, and he knew I would quickly tire from it, so he suggested that we go to his place and talk in a more quiet atmosphere." Lela's pulse began to race. "So, I, thinking it was okay and I really wanted to get out of there, left with him. I kept thinking, it's okay, he's never hurt me before, and it will be ok."

Tristan watched as tears formed and fell from Lela's eyes.

"So we got to his place and he locked the door behind him. That's not unusual ... who doesn't lock their doors when their at home. So I ignored it, then he turned down the lights... I ignored it. We sat on his couch, a couch that I had sat on many time before, and he started talking about how we belonged together and how I should be treating him with more respect and that I needed to learn what it is a real man needs. I figured he was just venting, so I told him, what he needed was to leave me alone and that I was leaving. But he wouldn't let me leave." Lela's voice softened to almost a whisper. "I won't go into how he did it, that fact is he raped me. This wasn't a man I didn't know or a complete stranger off the street. This was a man I had dated for seven months, a man who asked me to marry him." Her voice trailed off.

"Did you report it?"

"Yes."

"What happened?"

"He was arrested. He pled guilty and got fifteen years, but I recently found out that he got an early parole."

"When?"

"A few weeks ago… the man is free."

"No wonder you were scared when I came in. I'm so sorry."

"It's okay Tristan, stop apologizing." Lela bit her bottom lip.

"Did you ever tell your parents?"

"I didn't tell anyone except my pastor and my counseling group. I've been in counseling for over three years. Of course, people from school knew about it."

"Your group mates?"

"I used to co-host a victim's group meeting at my church bi-weekly. I haven't been there lately."

Tristan was overcome, and didn't know how to respond.

"How did you cope?" she finally asked.

"I didn't, I got angry." Lela stood and crossed her living room, headed toward the kitchen, "Do you want some lemonade?"

Tristan followed.

"Sure, if it's not too much trouble." Tristan sat at the kitchen table and watched as Lela filled two tall glasses with ice and lemonade.

"I hated men. I thought they were all liars. Every time I saw a man or spoke to one, I would wonder if he was going to rape me. It took me a long time to come to grips with what happened."

"But you're okay now?"

"I'm better than I was three years ago. I wouldn't leave my apartment without having someone with me; and my relationship with God suffered."

Seeing that the drinks were low Lela poured fresh drinks

into the glasses and took a seat directly across from Tristan.

"How?"

"Wow, you've got a lot of questions." Lela sighed. Tristan watched her as she fought to get the words out; each one more difficult than the other.

"I became resentful. I would not pray or go to church. I was numb."

"When did you decide to go to counseling?" Tristan sipped her lemonade.

"I didn't, it found me. In Colorado it was recommended by a school counselor but when I moved back home I start going to a new church because I didn't want anyone I knew asking me a lot of questions. I was running from myself and anyone who knew me. I finally got tired and had a breakdown during alter call."

"In front of everybody?"

"Some people had to carry me out. They let me sleep on a couch in one of the offices. The pastor and his wife woke me up a few hours later, apparently I needed the sleep. And that's when I told him what happened and I've been going to see him ever since."

"Maybe I should go to counseling. I need some serious guidance."

"It took me a long time to start talking to God again…" she got quiet, "…but I know now He never left me."

"You should tell Jake. Be as open and up front as possible. It will eliminate all doubt."

"This isn't about doubt, this is about my personal space and when I choose to allow someone that close to me. Besides, I want to tell him, but right now I just can't." Lela sighed, "You know I never knew how much I missed him until he came back."

"But you dated other men in the past, so why is this any different?"

"I was putting on airs, making myself look good so no one would ever question my happiness."

"How would dating do that?"

"People are dumb. They figure, oh she's dating, so she must be better. They think that if you have someone in your life, you can't be sad."

"I know what that's like."

Lela noticed that her laundry basket was in front of her laundry room door adjacent to her kitchen. She left her drink and picked up the basket as she entered her laundry room.

"I pray..." She called back to Tristan. "I pray all the time that I can be normal again. I *wish* my biggest problem was to avoid temptation, but it's not." Lela smiled through her tears. "It's easier when I'm not interested in a guy... no one is around to fall in love with or start to have feelings for, but I have come face-to-face with my first love and I want to love again."

Tristan listened. She had never known that Lela struggled so much. She decided to play devil's advocate.

"Scared?" Tristan watched from the laundry room door as Lela loaded her washing machine with clothes that had accumulated over the week.

"Why should I be?"

She hated when Lela acted oblivious, it was a bad habit that she was always trying to break.

"He might reject you."

"I don't think he'll do that."

"You seem so sure of yourself." Tristan paused. "You shouldn't be so cocky," she mumbled.

Lela was confused. Tristan seemed to be talking more to herself than to her.

"I'm not being cocky." Lela slid past her friend to re-enter the kitchen from the laundry room, and sat down at the kitchen table in front of her glass of lemonade. As if she were suspicious, she eyed her glass, glaring into the murky yellow liquid.

"I'll have to tell him sooner or later," Lela sighed. "But when the time is right."

"But he might reject you, if you tell him," Tristan pressed.

Lela kept her eyes on her glass.

"We're not married, if he wants to go, he can go."

"You say that now, but you know very well, you don't want him to leave."

"I thought you were encouraging me to be open with him a second ago. What's happened to that? Why are you so opposed to this now?"

"You're like the sister I never had and I love you. I just want to be sure you are basing your decisions on the right reasons."

Tristan was sincere and after her argument with Jeff, she wanted Lela and Jake to make it, even if it meant keeping something from him. But she knew that would not be right.

"I'm telling him the truth, just not right away. I need time," Lela replied.

"Mmmm. So are you going to tell him about those magic pills too?"

Lela rolled her eyes.

"He knows I take them."

"Yes, but does he know why and how long and how often and that you can't stop."

"So, I'm that transparent?"

"Anyone who can swallow pills without water or a second thought, like you did, when I walked in here, has either been on medication for a very long time or has a problem. I'm guessing both."

"Ummm."

"So what are they for?"

"Anxiety."

"How long?"

"Since the rape."

"Damn Lela… No one should be on pills that long."

"I know. But I need them."

"Keep telling yourself that. You're going to end up in an early grave. I bet that's why you couldn't even hear the alarm."

"Okay, fine. You want to hear that I abuse my medication, then fine. I abuse it. I take way more than I should and I've been taking them far longer than originally prescribed but my symptoms are still here."

"Then I know that you know that if your symptoms are still

here, then those pills are not working and you're still avoiding the real issues." Tristan left her post by the door and sat across from Lela.

"You're supposed to be on my side."

"I am. That's why I'm telling you this. Do you even know how many of those things you down a day?"

Lela hung her head. "I lose count."

"You should throw them away."

"I need-"

"Yeah, I know, you need them." Tristan interrupted. "Or at lest you think you do."

Since they were sharing secrets, Tristan felt it was time to share hers. "Okay, I'll get off your back."

Her secret was creeping out of shadows and haunting every action and decision that she made. It was a warrior, hell bent on revealing its truth. She fought her own emotions for self-preservation and fought to keep her delusion alive. But now, her friendship with Lela was tearing down her fortified walls.

"I never told you this, but Jeff and I, we didn't wait to have sex until we were married."

Lela giggled, causing her to hiccup, "Girl, I knew that already." She was happy that Tristan decided to put the spotlight on herself.

"You did!"

"You married a playa."

"That doesn't mean we were sleeping together."

"In whose world? That man was good at getting into panties."

"As I recall, so was Jake."

"Yes, he was, just not mine. Besides in the end he decided to live for God. He has become everything I've always wanted."

"So, why don't you tell him that?"

"I already explained that."

"Ok, I understand that you have been through a lot. But you can try, just take it slow. See where it goes."

"Slow... I like how that sounds.

Lela excused herself from the kitchen to use the bathroom.

Tristan placed her lemonade in the sink and went back into the living room. As she passed a book case she noticed a family album. She it picked up and sat down on the sofa and turned the pages admiring the family photographs of Lela and her parents. She was an only child and her parents doted on her. Tristan came across a picture of their graduation photo. She, Jake, Lela and Jeff posed in front of a statue of their school mascot. They were all grinning, holding their diplomas high; in yellow robs and caps. Another person in the photograph caught her eye. Off to the side, Leland stood holding the hand of a cropped out individual. *I wish it were that easy,* Tristan thought. *We were so naïve.*

"Ah memories." Lela walked in and saw Tristan viewing the album. "It's good to reminisce sometimes."

"Um. I wish mine were more on the smoother side."

"No matter what, you learn from them."

"Not me." Tristan flipped to a picture of her and Jeff inside his father's church. He was wearing a black suit with a deep maroon tie. "And certainly not Jeff."

"What are you talking about?"

"If you haven't noticed Jeff isn't doing too well these days."

"Is he drinking?"

"He says he's not, but at the dinner, he had to have slipped and had something or else he wouldn't have been acting that way..." She paused, "and lately he has become so aggressive."

"Have you talked to him about it?"

"Every time I try, he lashes out at me. That's another reason why I really wanted Jake to come over. I thought he might be able to help."

"What about your pastor or any one at your church?"

"You know as well as I do, that it's so hard to find an empathetic ear that won't turn around and gossip about what you've told them. I would go to our pastor, but I haven't even been to church in months... and Jeff has given it up all together."

"What do you mean?"

"I tried to get him to go with me a while back and he told me my faith was unreasonable and that God wasn't real." Tristan closed the album and placed it beside her, keeping her hand on its cover.

"But he was raised in the church, his father is a minister."

"That was then. He has had so many rough patches since then."

"Like what?"

"His mother's death."

"Umm, I heard."

"What you didn't hear was that she committed suicide." Lela's mouth dropped. Tristan moved in closer as if someone else was in the room and could hear.

"What happened?" Lela inquired.

"Jeff's mother struggled with depression, brought on by emotional abuse. Now you know why Jeff has a chip on his shoulder and why when Jake decided to convert, he and Jeff just didn't see eye to eye anymore." Tristan sighed. "Jeff can't distinguish between his father and a true man of God. Now, compound that with the fact that Jeff has known Jake all his life and knows all his dirty business."

"Well, so does everyone else, these days." Lela smirked.

A knock on the door interrupted their conversation. Lela excused herself and went to the door. She looked through her peep hole, only to find Jake on the other side.

"Who is it?" Tristan yelled over to Lela, upon seeing a blank look come across her friend's face.

"It's me." Jake answered from outside after hearing the question, although he didn't recognize the voice.

Tristan silently mimed to Lela to open to door, her arms wild and exuberant. Lela mouthed her unwillingness to comply and begged her to answer the door on her behalf.

"Hello. Is anyone there?" Jake had grown weary from the silence, although he could hear some movement. "Lela, are you there?"

Lela's eyes grew large and she rushed into her office and closed the door behind her. She stood in the darkness, listening as Tristan opened the door and greeted Jake.

"Hey, what are you doing here?" he asked somewhat confused.

"I was visiting."

"Where's Lela?"

Tristan hesitated in answering as she didn't want to lie to a minister, but she didn't want to force Lela into a corner, either.

"Well, she's indisposed right now."

"So, she's here." Jake felt like he was getting the run around

"Yeah," Tristan breathed. "But like I said she's busy."

"If she's busy, why are you still here?" Jake looked her in the eyes.

"I'm..." Tristan looked around trying to avoid his eyes. "I'm just leaving actually... So that she could be alone."

"Tristan, you're horrible at lying."

Tristan huffed at the accusation, despite its truth. Then she dug her heels into the floor.

"She's in her office," she whispered

Lela strained to hear what she was saying. "She doesn't want to see you right now."

"Why?" Jake whispered following Tristan's cue. "I'm here to apologize."

"There's a lot she has to tell you, and she's afraid you won't understand or that you might judge her, or run away."

"If I was going to run, I would have by now. Can you tell me what's happening?"

"It's not my place. Besides, it's a long story that I'm not equipped to tell."

Finally, frustrated from not being able to overhear their conversation, Lela thrust open the door from her office and saw Jake and Tristan standing beside the entrance, with the front door wide open.

"You're letting all my air out. Do you mind?"

Jake reached behind him and closed the door, keeping his eyes on Lela. She was dressed in white cotton from head to toe and her hair in a wrap. He could not move his eyes off of her. Tristan realized she was now a third wheel and eased behind Jake.

"Tristan, where are you going?" Lela asked.

"Home. You two have some things to discuss."

"No, we don't."

"Lela, I know you're scared, but sooner or later you have to start trusting someone. Why not him?" She had over stepped her bounds, but she knew it would be alright. "So, I'll call you."

With that, she left the two standing in the foyer. Tristan was happy to be a part of bringing together two people who really needed each other, but as soon as she got in her car dread began to fill her spirit. She now had to face her own husband. How was she going to tell him the truth about their marriage and that he was not the only liar.

# Chapter Eighteen
## What's Hidden

Jake took a step toward Lela which caused her to move suddenly, knocking over an oversized flower vase that was placed on a table in her foyer. Both saw it was going to spill over and dived to grab it before it hit the ground. Jake managed to catch it, but also managed to get drenched in the process from the water that poured all over the suit he was still wearing from the day's work.

"Oh my goodness, you're soaking wet."

"It will dry."

"You don't want that to dry. It will ruin your suit."

"It's just water."

"No, it's not, I put other stuff in there. Take off your clothes."

"Excuse me." Jake stammered.

"You know what I mean. I'm going to clean it."

"And what am I supposed to wear."

"I have a robe you can put on."

"I'm not wearing a woman's robe."

"Stop it." Lela laughed, "It's just me, for goodness sake. Go in my bathroom and change. I'll look around maybe I have something else." Not wanting to go back and forth, Jake went into Lela's bathroom and took off his wet clothes. Lela managed to find an old sweatshirt and pajama pants in a box she had picked up from her parents that she was supposed to drop off at Goodwill. She knocked on her bathroom door.

"Here are some clothes."

"No girly stuff."

"I promise." Lela giggled. Jake opened the door enough for Lela to slide the clothes through. Lela leaned against the wall and grinned, thinking about Jake in his vulnerable state.

Lela felt her stomach calling for attention and she was in no mood to cook "Do you want something to eat? I can order some Chinese food," she yelled.

"Ah, sure…"

While Jake dressed, called and ordered more than enough food for the two of them. Moments after, Jake emerged from her bedroom un-amused by his appearance.

"Don't laugh at me."

"It's kind of hard not to."

"Yeah I know." He chuckled. "Did you order?"

"Yes."

The room began to get dark as the sun set. Lela went to her window and closed her curtains, then began to light her wall candles. Lela preferred candles to lights, as they weren't as harsh on her eyes. The walls glowed from the every angle. Jake watched her as she moved swiftly from one candle to another, and when she was satisfied she sat down on her sofa and reached for her throw blanket and covered herself.

"What would your parishioners say about you now?" Lela giggled. "You're in my home late at night, undressed and in someone else's clothes."

"Well, like I've said before, it's nobody's business and besides there's nothing going on." Jake paused. "Is there?"

"No."

"Well then… we have nothing to worry about, except our friendship."

"Are you worth it?" she asked. "Because sometimes it's just easier not to be friends."

Jake went to sit beside her on the sofa.

"I think I am and I know you are, but I understand your apprehension."

"It seems silly that we couldn't at least be friends. We've known each other for forever."

"Yeah, so start filling me in on what it is that has been bothering you. Friend."

"All of it?"

"All of it, Lela." He was serious.

"You first."

"You still don't trust me?"

"I need to know why you are the man you are now. It may seem stupid to you, but to me it will help me to decide whether we can be friends in passing or friends forever."

"So, it comes to this."

"I have to protect myself. If I don't, who will?"

"God will."

"Tell me, Jake." She said it with finality.

"I think my head is going to explode." He started. "Long story short, I was a whore of man and I woke up one day next to some woman I didn't know, and had no idea where she came from."

"Yikes."

"Yeah, that's about the only word for it." He paused. "Do you want me to continue?"

"Please do."

"It freaked me out and I began to question what my life was about. If this was all it was worth."

"Screwing strangers?" Lela was shocked by her own words. So was Jake, who looked at her with a whole new light.

"Lela, why so vulgar?"

"I don't know what came over me, sorry."

"Jealous."

"Hardly." She rolled her eyes.

"Maybe I shouldn't tell you the rest."

"No, look." Lela shook her head. "I'm sorry. I confess it's hard for me to hear that you have been with women. I guess on some obscure level I am... jealous."

"Don't be. I didn't care for any of those women, I was acting out."

The door bell rang.

"That must be the food."

"I'll get it."   Jake jumped up and retrieved the food, returning in very little time.  After setting a place to eat, the two settled back into their seats.  Jake watched as Lela delicately ate her food and chewed it slowly.

"I don't want to be just your friend.  Ever."

His words ran through her body and awakened her spirit. His voice was passionate and even though he had not moved from his place, she felt as if he were pulling her towards him with a magnet.  It was an unknown feeling and it terrified her to her very core.

"Continue with your story."   She decided to ignore his comment.

He knew she was retreating, but did not want to press her.

"I was at work one day and one of my colleagues, who's a minister, invited me to attend his church."

"Did you go?"

"No.  I lied and told him I would, but ended up with some girl that night instead."

Lela was intrigued and hung on every word.

"Well, I woke up the next morning and I felt totally empty.  I started having nightmares of dying alone.  I would wake up in cold sweats in the middle of the night and to ease my fear and shame I started drinking.  A few months passed and I got a call from the young lady that I had slept with that night and she invited me to go to church.  She told me she had to hunt me down…" he paused.  "Then she told me she was HIV positive."

Lela stopped eating and placed her food down.  She saw Jake's mouth tighten as he rubbed the back of his head.

"I was totally ashamed and scared out of my mind.  She told me I needed to be tested, and apologized to me.  I spiraled into a depression.  I missed work and drank heavily.  I didn't get tested because I was afraid of what the outcome would be." Jake stood up and walked over to the fireplace.  "One night I stopped by a local liquor store and bought the largest bottle of tequila I could find.  I drove home, drinking the whole way. How I made it to my apartment without harming anyone had to be by the grace of God."  Jake looked at Lela, and continued.

"When I got home I wanted to just feel something... so I opened a drawer, grabbed a knife..." Jake paused and pulled up his sleeves to reveal scaring on his wrist. Lela gasped at the sight and stood up to be face to face with him. She touched the scars with her fingertips and tears started to form in her eyes.

"You didn't?" She frowned

"I did. I sliced my wrist wide open." Tears began to flow down Jake's face. "God saved me from suicide and he saved me from HIV. I tested negative while I was in the hospital, soon after I came to Christ." Jake watched Lela as she gazed at his scars lightly touching them. She took his hand in hers, holding it tightly.

"I'm so happy you're here."

"I am, too." Jake looked her in the eyes, her expressions had softened. She smiled slightly.

"Your turn." He waited.

Lela stepped back from him, knowing it was time. Not wanting to belabor what happened, she blurted it out.

"I was raped."

Jake's face fell, and Lela watched as he silently expressed his emotions, from shock, to confusion, to anger, then rage. Jake did not say a word, he flexed his hands-- closing and opening them continuously. Lela observed his reaction; she had not expected such an emotional response.

"Are you okay?" Jake asked.

"It happened years ago, so physically, I'm fine now, but I do have the occasional panic attack."

"Is that why you take the pills?"

Lela bit the inside of her cheek. "Yes."

"So, emotionally, you're still hurting."

"I'm talking to you, which I would not have done a week ago."

"Yes but..."

"Okay, don't do that."

"Do what?"

"Don't feel sorry for me or treat me like I'm... like I, can't take care of myself."

"I don't mean to do that, I'm just worried." Jake hesitated. "What happened to the guy?"

"He went to jail, but he's out now on parole."

"Was it someone you knew?"

"The guy I told you about, the guy who asked me to marry him."

Jake now understood Lela's uneasy behavior and unwillingness to be close to anyone, especially him. He sat down in the arm chair and leaned back. Lela followed his lead, returning to her sofa. The two sat in silence for what seemed a long time. Lela wondered what he was thinking, but was unsure if she should ask. Finally the silence became deafening.

"What are you thinking?"

"It's my fault; I never should have left you."

"It was not your fault. It was a bad thing that happened, but it was not my fault and certainly was not yours."

Jake shook his head in disbelief.

"I don't know what to say."

"You don't have to say anything. It is what it is."

"So, this is why you don't want to be friends."

"I want you as my friend, Jake. I just can't handle anything else. I'm afraid I could never please you." Lela felt her face begin to heat up.

"Please me?" Jake gasped. "What do you mean? What is it you think I want from you?"

"Oh, come on. Eventually you will want to get married. Marriage means intimacy, and I don't know if I can handle that."

"You mean spiritually, you were afraid to let me in emotionally."

"Yes." She paused, "and physically." Lela tears began to flow.

Jake moved closer to Lela, wrapping his arms around her. She tried to back away, but was so desperate for his touch that she allowed him to comfort her. He pulled her close and she leaned against his shoulder and seemed to sink into him. Jake had missed her and he knew what it meant to search for something and never find it. She had searched for understanding and love and he searched for inner peace. Before his conversion he made the mistake of trying to find peace in material things and women, only to find that nothing compared to the purity of the relationship he had with Lela. He missed her.

"I'm sorry…"

"Please don't." The moment was all too surreal and unrealistic for her. "Your clothes should be ready by now, you should go."

Lela broke away from Jake's hug and stood up. Jake not wanting to leave for fear of being pushed away again, followed her.

"Jake you should go." She whimpered half-heartedly. He ignored her attempt at rejection and embraced her once again. Holding her head in his hand he wiped away her tears. There they stood; Lela felt his hands cupping her face as his fingers wiped her tears. They were strong, but soft; and for the first time in years, she wasn't afraid, his touch didn't make her fill threatened or dirty. On compulsion Jake brought his lips close to hers. He hesitated and looked in her eyes for some sign of approval before giving in completely. Lela allowed his gentle touch and found herself wrapping her arms around his broad shoulders. Jake was surprised to find that after all these years his influence was still strong, but he knew was wrong for imposing it. Although trying to suppress his thoughts to stop, his conscience was yelling for him to cease. Lela had always sparked a passion in him that had the potential to become uncontrollable.

Lela found herself indulging in the kiss, gradually allowing it to build in intensity. She didn't want the feeling to stop. She felt safe, but in the pit of her stomach, she felt a nagging that urged her to back away before it could not be managed. In the midst of an overwhelming urge, Jake pulled away. He breathed heavily and was almost in tears as he made his way toward the door.

"I should go." Jake kept his eyes toward the floor as not to make any more attempts of direct eye contact.

"But your clothes…" She didn't want him to leave

"I'll pick them up another time."

"I'm sorry, forgive me." She said softly.

"You didn't do anything wrong. You asked me to leave and I kissed you instead. I should be asking for your forgiveness. This was not why I came here today." Jake opened the door and stood in the threshold.

"Wasn't it? I mean you do want a relationship."

"A relationship, yes. A friendship, yes. I don't want to ever be out of control." Jake eyes were sparkling. "I want you to trust me, trust that I will never take advantage of you." His eyes pleaded with her.

"I do." Lela nodded her head and stood next to him, reached over and gently ran her fingers down the back of his head to his neck. He was not Michael, he would not betray her.

# Chapter Nineteen
### Inspired

After Jake left, Lela was besieged with inspiration, so she quickly picked up a pad and pen and let her thoughts flood the pages before her.

*Everyone has a story. There are people who have had what I would call an over and abundantly blessed life and I have to say I have been one of them. But this life did not come without its struggles.*

Lela had decided that the best way to take control of her fears was to tell her story. She grabbed her phone and dialed Joyce's number.

"Hello, Lela! It's late. What's wrong?"

"Nothing's wrong, Joyce, I have news."

"You sound excited, so tell."

"I have a new idea for a book ... my biography, my story."

"But we have already put so much work into this one, can't the new idea wait?"

"No, Joyce. Just listen to my story, take it to your supervisors. I will run with whatever you come back with."

"That's fair. So tell me. What makes your life story different from any other?"

Jake arrived home just after eleven in the evening. His apartment was small, but adequate for his needs. He sat down on his couch, one of the few items he had in his apartment. It was a barren space. He didn't need much, and was blessed to have mentors who gave him their hand-me-down clothes. Jake didn't make much money, just enough to pay his essentials, so he saved the rest. He was dedicated to saving and was efficient at regulating his funds. It was the one trait he always had. Jake had not planned on ever owning a home, until he saw Lela again. He knew in the moment he fell in love with her again that he wanted more for himself. Her mere presence in his life was motivating him to want a home and family. He believed it would come in time, but he had not expected her to have so much painful baggage in her life. Though, it did not deter him from his desire. He didn't know how to handle the news of her violation, so he decided to call his pastor. Even though it was late, he knew he would still be up. His pastor immediately knew who it was by the caller ID.

"What's up, son?"

"Hey. Sorry to call so late."

"You know it's not a problem."

"The woman I told you about, well we finally talked."

"That's great, how did it go?"

"I told her my testimony, she told me hers. But I didn't expect what I heard."

"Well, I don't need to know the details, because it sounds like something that needs to stay between the two of you, and you sound overwhelmed."

"I love her. I always have. I don't want to ever hurt her. She has been hurt so much already and I don't ever want to add to that."

"You have a desire to do what is right and you know her well. You might want to consider just being there for her, if that is all you can do right now. A committed relationship may not be what is in your, or her, best interest."

"I feel so inept. As if there is nothing I can do to help her. Maybe I should just back off all together."

"Does she want you to back off?"

"No, she told me not to."

"Then do what she asks. Be her friend, be her prayer partner but don't walk away. No matter what, know that in every relationship there is going to be a trial. Coming from a married man, you must never walk away; a man stays in the thick of it."

"Come hell or high water."

"Come hell or high water, or storm, through sickness and in health. Seriously, if you are looking to marry this woman, the responsibility and commitment to stay and be present in her life as man of God starts now. You need to show her you want this, so be consistent, be patient, and be clear about your intentions."

"I get it." Jake stared at a photograph he had of Lela. He had pulled it out of his trunk after he saw her again at the wedding. Not wanting to put it back, he framed it and placed it on his wall. The picture was taken in her freshman year of college, and not long after, he broke up with her. She was smiling, standing on the beach wearing jeans and a tank top. Her jeans were soaked at her feet from standing in the water, but she wasn't fazed. *She hasn't changed*, he thought. *She's just hiding within herself.*

"Jake, you still there?"

"Yeah, sorry."

"It's okay. How about you bring your friend over for dinner some time?"

"Sure, I'll ask her about it."

"Good."

Saved for a Season

# Chapter Twenty
## Wavering

Tristan saw Lela roll her eyes before she could even ask how the beaded blue v-neck blouse looked on her.

"What? This one, too?" Tristan pouted. "But it's my size."

"Size is not the problem, style is," Lela answered.

The three women had managed to squeeze some shopping into their schedules, followed by dinner and a movie.

"I agree." Camille popped her head up from a clearance rack that was filled with dresses. "It's just too much."

"What do you mean? It's only thirty bucks," Tristan replied, frustrated. This was the fourth blouse she had tried on and none of them worked.

"I don't mean the price, silly. I mean all that beadwork and shimmer and glitter. Girl, please find something else," Camille answered.

It was amazing that Camille and Tristan were able to go a whole afternoon without arguing, but since they had it out at the dinner party, they had been doing better and even made attempts to hang out with each other, but usually with a third person around.

"No, I give up. I'll just stick with this dress." Tristan held up a silk black wrap dress, with lace detail.

"Not bad." Lela remarked. " Now, can we go and eat? I'm ravished."

The three women paid for their items, left the store and loaded their purchases into their respective vehicles after deciding that it was best that they drive separately since they all would go in different directions once the evening was over. Once they arrived at the restaurant, they were seated in a booth and ordered drinks. They chose a bistro that was intimate and had a familial appeal. The food was pricey but well presented and available in whatever serving size you requested, as long as it was reasonable.

"I love this place." Camille beamed.

"Yeah, they have the best variety of tea I have ever seen," Tristan chimed in.

Lela was silent. She didn't go out much and it was very rare that she ate out, unless it was with her parents. She spent most of the time listening to the two sisters gab about work, husbands and children. It was then that Lela realized how much farther ahead her friends were in life and relationships. If they weren't married, they were engaged and many had children. She felt left behind.

"I should have never married him," Camille admitted to Tristan. "He was your boyfriend first anyway. I should have known it was a mistake from the beginning."

"Is that your way of apologizing for taking him from me?" Tristan asked.

"No, you two weren't together at that time and you said you were finished with him. I understand that I violated some rule about dating your sister's first and all but I didn't go after him while you two were dating and it surely wasn't intentional."

Tristan rolled her eyes. "Not intentional?"

"Well, no."

"Are you two going to go through this again? Because if you are, I don't want to sit through it." Lela stared at the two from across the table. "I mean really, who cares now? Neither of you want him."

"That's true." Tristan agreed but Camille just nodded her head.

"I know that I have done a lot of things that weren't good, and I probably deserve a load of the bad things to come my way," Camille paused. "But when does the struggle stop?"

Lela and Tristan looked at each other, puzzled.

"What do you mean?" Lela finally asked.

"I don't really know."

"I know, kind of," Tristan spoke up. "It's like you have this expectation for your life and what it should be. Not by any fault of your own, but it's an expectation that was given to you from your parents or friends."

"Yeah." Camille turned to her. "Like we should have a certain kind of life or even just a certain kind of expectation of happiness, but no one tells you the truth."

"What truth?" Lela asked.

"That those expectations aren't for everybody. That grand life that everyone seems to reach for cannot be attained by everyone and that more likely than not, you will do something stupid to mess it up."

"Like what?"

"Like, tell a horrible lie that you can't take back," Camille rattled.

"Or cheat," Tristan added.

"So you two are talking about marriage expectations."

"Life, too." Tristan nodded.

"Sometimes it's just too hard to face your mistakes," Lela acknowledged.

"And what mistakes have you made?" Tristan asked.

"I have my list, which I choose not to share."

"Always the secretive one."

"It's not that I can't tell, it's just that I don't want to." Then Lela added, "Besides, with Camille around they would just end up in Ms. Sutter's ear and then the whole world would know all my dirt."

The girls laughed, even Camille who was able to take a joke.

"So, when are you going to take the plunge?" Camille asked.

Lela placed her hot cup of earl gray tea down and fiddled with an empty pack of sugar.

"Plunge into what?" Lela asked.

"Marriage, silly." Camille elbowed her sister for help, but Tristan just picked up her own cup of tea and pretended to be consumed with its aroma, some blend of African berries and lemon.

"I really don't have a clue," Lela answered. "And by the state of your marriages, I would probably do well not to."

"Well, now that you and *minister-man* are together, you must have some idea." Camille was persistent.

Tristan raised an eyebrow, continuing to pretend she was uninterested in the conversation, but clearly she was.

"Together." Lela cleared her throat. "What do you mean, together?"

"You know," Camille smiled broadly. "You two are dating, everyone knows you are."

"What?" Lela was as surprised as anyone.

"Well, according to Ms. Sutter, you and Jake are a real item and so very close to tying everything down." Camille fluttered her eyes lashes in assurance of her gossip. "And you know Ms. Sutter would know."

"What!" Lela laughed at the idea. "We are not even close to marriage. I mean…" She fumbled, then added, "We're not even a couple. I mean, not really."

"You don't seem to know what you mean," Tristan murmured.

"You should talk." Lela glared at Tristan as she hung her head.

"Don't turn this around on me," Tristan shot back.

"What exactly are you waiting for?" Camille dug deeper.

"Yeah, what *are* you waiting for?" Tristan bit her lip quickly and inwardly kicked herself. Camille smiled widely, finally help, she thought.

"I'm not waiting for anything!" she said defensively, and then looked crossly at Tristan who was pretending to be deeply interested in the dessert menu. "I am simply saying, we are not a couple. We are just friends."

Camille laughed and elbowed Tristan again. "She's lying thru her teeth and it's not attractive."

"Would you stop that! That hurts." Tristan wiggled away from her sister's elbow jab.

"Oh, come on." Camille continued to laugh and turned her head back and forth between Tristan and Lela but finally ended on Lela again. "You two are so perfect for each other." Her voice became wistful and romantic as if she were reciting lines from a Jane Austin classic. "Here he is the brooding handsome pastor, waiting patiently for his long lost virgin love to give herself to him."

"Maybe we should talk about something else." Tristan rolled her eyes in agony as her sister embarrassed herself. She fought the urge to slap her.

"Nonsense." Camille waved away Tristan's suggestion and continued in her storyteller narration. "And here you are, the daydreaming beauty, waiting for prince charming to come and sweep you off your feet and rediscover the fire that smolders in hidden places inside you, as both of you silently admire each other from afar."

Tristan and Lela could barely believe their ears and were grateful for the arrival of the waitress with their food. But food did not stop Camille.

"I hope you two don't waste time on past foolishness."

"We aren't wasting our time on anything, Camille. We're not a couple."

"You're definitely not a couple?" Tristan asked. "Then why does he visit you so much?"

"Ohhhh." Camille covered her mouth in anticipation of an answer. "Now this is good, this is good dirt, do tell. He visits? Does the man," she paused for affect, "*stay*?"

"What! No." Lela stiffened in disbelief of the question. "No... No. Never!"

"Ummmm she's blushing."

"She is." Tristan giggled.

The women laughed again. "So you two haven't even kissed?" Camille pried.

"Wait, what?" Lela stammered. "Why does this matter?"

"They have!" Camille yelped and dropped her fork.

"Why didn't you tell me? You heifer," Tristan said in shock.

"What? Wait-"

"No tell me… when did this happen?"

"Yes… dish it, girl!" Camille leaned in. "Was it good?"

"Was it lingering?"

"Did he put his in tongue in your mouth?"

"Did you put your tongue in his?" Again the two sisters broke into laughter.

"You two are gross." Lela gave in with laughter.

"Okay, really." Tristan leaned in. "Did you?"

"A lady never kisses and tells."

"Bull! Now tell," Camille ordered.

Lela hesitated for a moment. She wanted to share like a true friend would, but knew that Camille would never keep it to herself. Finally, her need for girl talk won out and she caved. "We did, a while ago."

The sisters were filled with delight and giggled. "Tell us more."

Lela blushed, "Well… his lips are softer than rose petals."

"Was it the same as when you were teenagers?" Tristan asked

"Goodness, I hope not. Boys don't know what they are doing when they're teenagers," Camille stated. "Go on."

"Well, no. Although he was good when we were younger, he was much better now. It's like we were drawn to each other, it just kind of happened and then we went our separate ways."

"You what!" Camille sat back. "That's all … no that can't be all … not from Jake."

"Sorry, to disappoint you but Jake really is no longer the player. He didn't try me at all."

"I can't believe it. So, Pastor Jake, really is, Pastor Jake."

"Yes. He is a gentleman and completely respectable."

"Ummm." Camille seemed slightly impressed. "So people can change."

"Yes."

"So, you kissed him but you're not a couple."

"We are friends, really good friends, but we are not a couple, right now."

"That's not how Ms. Sutter tells it." Camille pushed hard.

"Again, with Ms. Sutter. You know, she says a lot of things she shouldn't say," Lela pointed out.

"She really does, she needs a muzzle," Tristan chimed in. "And exactly what *did* Ms. Sutter say?"

"Before or after she finished talking about you?" Camille laughed. "Oh I'm just joking." But they all knew very well that she wasn't and Lela suddenly regretted sharing with Camille the details about her and Jake. "Well, she called me, to see how I was doing because of the divorce and everything.-"

"Out of the goodness of her nosy little heart," Tristan giggled.

"Anyway," Camille rolled her eyes. "She informed me that Mrs. Duval, the secretary at the church Jake is associate pastor at, told her that your Jake is quite smitten over you." Camille smiled broadly.

"Mrs. Duval, told Ms. Sutter this?"

"Yes."

"Who uses the word smitten, anymore?" Tristan interjected.

"I do," Camille answered.

"But it's so played."

"No, *played* is *played*. Smitten is forever."

"Okay, ya'll. Who cares? Really." Lela stopped them. "Why would Mrs. Duval say that to Ms. Sutter?"

"Because it's true," Camille said. "And because she heard it from the horse's mouth."

"Jake has been talking about me to other people?"

Tristan detected an annoyed tone in Lela's voice.

"I'm sure he wasn't saying anything inappropriate … just like you didn't say too much tonight," Tristan said.

"No, the mere fact that my name is coming out of his mouth to others is inappropriate. I knew better than to trust him."

"Trust him, "Camille gasped. "What's the big deal? So he mentioned that he liked you. That's a good thing. You just sat here and told us about kissing him."

"That's different… and you forced it out of me!" Lela said defensively, but she knew she was wrong. "What else is he mentioning?"

"Well, nothing," Camille answered, a bit thrown. "What else should he be mentioning?" Her eyebrow rose.

"Nothing," Lela hissed. Camille had gotten enough juicy gossip from her for the evening. "Look, I have to go." She pulled out her pocketbook and grabbed some cash.

"No, Lela. Stay. I am sure he didn't mention anything that would put you two at odds. He really does care about you." Tristan tried to reason with Lela but she was already flustered.

"I don't care." Lela breathed deeply. "I need some air. I have to go home."

She handed Tristan her cash for dinner and left the bistro. When she reached her car she sat inside for a while before starting the vehicle. *Am I overreacting*, she thought. *No, I know him, if he talked about liking me, then he has told somebody my secret. Damn it!* She hit the top of the steering wheel. *It's my story to tell, not his!* As she sat there contemplating her next move, her cell phone rang. Caller ID indicated it was Jake.

"What do you want?" she answered furiously.

"Whoa, what? Who answers a phone like that?"

"I do, when a blabber mouth is on the other end. Did you really have to go and tell people about what happened to me?"

"Wait, what?" Jake was confused. "I didn't tell anyone... I mean, not about what happened to you. Not really."

"Not really, Jake. What the hell does that mean?"

"It means I didn't tell anyone about what happened to you in Colorado."

"I was raped, Jake."

"I know that."

"Say it."

"Say what?"

"Say it! You're afraid to say it."

"Fine, you were raped," he said breathlessly, and added, "But I didn't tell anyone you were raped." He didn't like hearing the words, much less repeating them. He didn't like the idea of some man imposing himself on her and didn't like that she forced him to say it.

"Great, now that you've said it and it is fully clear to you, maybe you will leave me alone."

"What?"

"Alone, Jake, I can't do this, I thought maybe I could... for just one moment maybe it was possible but now I know I can't and you will thank me someday for sparing you the heartache."

"Sparing me!"

Lela could hear the heat in his voice.

"Are you kidding me? I'll tell you when I want to be spared Lela, and it is not now. I told you, I wanted you and I meant it. That means all the history and all the baggage that comes with it. So, you better get used to me be being around, because no matter how you act or how you try and push me away, I'm not going anywhere. I will be here. I was a fool and lost you once, I will not lose you again. And yes, I talked about you, to my Pastor. I told him, how much I was falling in love with you and how much I wanted to communicate with you and be there for you ...and that was it, nothing else. I would never betray your trust. Period!" Jake's head spun. "I love you Lela." His voice softened. "And that's all there is to it."

The silence on the phone was deafening. Jake could still hear Lela breathing on the other end, but didn't know if any of his words got through.

"I'm sorry. But I don't think I'm ready for this," she finally spoke. She could hear Jake sigh heavily. "I'm scared, Jake." Her voice quivered.

"I am, too," he answered. "But I'm not running."

"It's not about that. You expect too much from me. I mean you're a pastor."

"So what?"

"So..." She tried to find her words. "So, that brings on responsibilities that I might not be ready for. Hell, I can barely be in places with my own family without feeling like my privacy has been infringed upon, not to mention getting involved with you."

"You won't have to worry about that."

"Of course I will. I'll have to worry that people are constantly judging everything I do and say."

"So, what's the difference between you writing your books and dating me?"

"Oh, don't even-" She cut him off.

"No, wait... don't what?" He was confused. "You've made your career by producing religious books that paint you as a person who has it all together. But you don't. You're so scared, you won't let those who love you in to get to know the real you. All of you, not just the pretty sides."

"It's my life... I live it as I want."

"What life Lela? You try your best to push everyone away. How can you write about God's love if you're not willing to show it to others in friendship, real friendship?"

""You see ... I knew this would happen. You do hold me to a higher standard. Well, I can't stand on your pedestal, Jake. I'm not that person, so forget about me!"

"Go ahead, Lela ...you can try to push me away, but I'm not going. I'll wait."

Lela hung up the phone.

# Chapter Twenty-One
## Something New?

After the night she had with Jake, Lela was not in the best mood for writing, but knew that the previous nights' events would only help fuel her story. She received an email that her new literary assistant would arrive at her home, bright and early that morning. She took another sip of her fizzy energy drink and straightened out her work space, then prepared a light breakfast in case the assistant might arrive hungry.

According to Joyce, the assistant came with excellent references and an incredible work ethic, which was going to be needed since Lela put her self-help book on the back burner to start her autobiography and her publisher wanted a finished work at the same deadline as her original work. It was risky and she could lose her advance if she failed, but it was also a risk allowing strangers to know intimate details of her life. This was a risk she was keen to take, despite what Jake thought, and a story she was ready to share.

Lela stayed up all night writing after she left Camille and Tristan at the restaurant. She had already filled three legal pads with her ideas and was running on pure adrenaline and dread-- an unusual combination for her. Usually, optimism was the driving force that kept her motivated and she was used to running on that emotion. She was used to feeding off of its intoxication. The door bell rang and she jumped with anticipation.

"Coming!" she yelled.

On the other side of the door stood a tall dark chocolate brotha' with bright round quarter eyes, wearing a scruffy gold-t.

"Lela?" he questioned "I'm Andrew Travis." He extended his left hand for a handshake. "The agency sent me." His voice was thick with a distinct accent. She knew it immediately.

"You're from Philly." She met his hand with hers. She noticed that he wasn't wearing a ring. Funny, she had never bothered to notice those things before.

"Yeah, how'd you guess?" He smiled brightly.

"I worked a summer internship up there while I was in school. It's a nice place."

"You mean it's the best place!" he quipped.

"Oh, yeah, of course, love that Philly ego. Come on in." Lela noticed his long stride as he followed her to the living room, where they would work.

She offered him some refreshments, which he gladly accepted and then they continued to make small talk. He talked about his final year in school. He was young, a mere twenty-two. Lela shared more about herself, and for some reason, felt free to talk about personal things with him. He didn't ask for details, but she gave them anyway. She soon turned to the rape and for a second thought about keeping it to herself, but that was silly because Andrew already knew. It was what the book was about. So, she continued and he listened, even taking notes.

"Did you get all that down?" she finally asked with a smirk. He knew she was joking but wanted to put her at ease.

"I don't want to forget anything and you never know what may be helpful to your book. By the way, I love your books... I mean wow! But this story is going to touch lives," He complimented.

She liked the way his mouth moved when he talked and found herself watching him, more than listening.

"What? Oh thanks." What was wrong with her? She shook herself, then picked up her legal pad. He took her cue and got his laptop in place. From there it was non- stop work. Andrew was ready, he didn't need coaxing, in fact he was a major help. He confidently threw out ideas and gave critiques without Lela seeking it. Their work flow was seamless.

While Lela's day began on a high note, unbeknown to Jake, his day was about to get rough. Already ten minutes late to a church board minutes, he rushed down the city streets. He could see the steeple of his church from a block away as he came to a complete stop at a stop sign. Jake didn't bother to look before he began to move forward, and suddenly he felt a sharp jolt throw his body forward, followed by a blast that pushed him back into his driver seat. The force knocked his breath out of his body and he sat motionless for what seemed an eternity. What had just happened?

After hours of tireless writing, Lela decided it was time for a break.

"Andrew, close that laptop. Let's grab lunch."

"Okay." Andrew saved his documents, then sat back in his chair. He watched as Lela strolled to the kitchen.

"Do you need any help?"

"No, I got it!" she yelled back.

"You sure? I'm pretty good in the kitchen." He walked over to the kitchen doorway and leaned against the wall. She had already pulled a dish from the refrigerator that looked like chicken salad and was in the process of cutting croissants in halves.

"Are you?" Lela turned and smiled back at him.

"Yeah, and that's not the only room I'm good in."

Lela couldn't believe her ears. Andrew was coming on to her. *No. That's not what he meant*, she thought. *Did he?*

"So what other rooms are you good in?" She decided to test him and see where he was coming from. He could have very well meant the boardroom, or an office, he *was* a writer.

"Well, I'm pretty good in front of a crowd. I do stand-up comedy some times."

Lela breathed in deep, glad she didn't jump to conclusions. But she knew he couldn't be interested in her, she was at least eight years his senior and he knew about what had happened to her, so there is no way, he would hit on her.

"But I am also pretty good in private shows." Andrew had

moved into the kitchen and stood beside Lela at the kitchen table.

Lela knew she wasn't hearing things. He was making a pass at her. That young thing was fishing. What should she say? She thought quickly.

"What type of shows?" *What was she saying!* She thought to herself. *Tell him to stop, tell him you're not interested, tell him you are damaged goods, tell him you're in love with another man, tell him the truth!* But she didn't know the truth anymore.

"The type that go on in bedrooms." He had answered assuredly.

"Andrew... I don't think."

"Why think at all?" he countered. "I think you've been doing so much thinking that you've forgotten what it feels like to be a woman."

"How dare you!"

"Don't be offended." He was calm and relaxed. "It's okay. I'm not looking for anything you don't want to give, but I don't mind being your experiment. I'm just saying, I won't take more than you're willing or ready to give."

"What?" Her head was swimming.

"I've read your work and now I see you in person and get to see how you work. Knowing your story, it's like you're a caged bird dying to be yourself but restricted because of one event. And I'm not trying to minimize it by any means. I'm just saying...." He paused. "You need to let it go, and know that every man who meets you is not going to think of that. What they are going to see is the woman you are."

"And what's that?" She was fixed on him, his voice, his words.

"Strong. Straight up and down. No bull. You are incredibly strong. To go through what you did and not be immeasurably messed up." He stepped toward her. "Not to mention, you're sexy as hell."

Lela stepped back and clinched the chair beside her. She looked around her kitchen, avoiding eye contact with Andrew. She felt something different than with Jake, and wondered for a second what it was. As frightening as it was to admit it, she knew what it was... She stood up straight and unclenched the chair, then looked Andrew in his eyes.

"So, what do you think we should do?"

"Whatever you want." He smiled.

He was exactly what she needed, or so she thought. He would ask nothing of her, expect nothing from her and still treat her like a sensual being. Jake didn't understand, so he tiptoed around her like she would break at any moment.

Andrew had no expectations of her. She stood in that kitchen for what seemed a lifetime, debating with herself. Would it be okay if she dabbled a little? Lela didn't know what she felt anymore but she knew she wanted to be held like a woman that a man found alluring and didn't pity; and Andrew was willing.

"Are you okay?" Jake heard someone screaming. The voice sounded like Lela's.

"Lela?" he asked.

"No, I'm Stacey. Tell me your name," she commanded.

"Jake," he murmured as he held his ribs.

"Jake, good. Good." She kept repeating herself. "Jake, you were hit by a car."

"What? But I wasn't even moving."

"Yeah, well, you're definitely not moving now."

"Bad joke," he said.

"Sorry."

Jake's eyes finally focused and he was able to see Stacey. She was an EMT. "You'll be okay though, but you definitely look like you have some rib damage. We're going to transport you to the hospital.

Jake moaned in anguish as they wheeled him into the ambulance. He saw the police taking statements and an officer escorted him to the hospital. He was somewhere between pain and numbness.

"Is there anyone you want us to contact?" The officer asked.

"My Pastor," he quickly stated, "And my girlfriend, Lela."

Saved for a Season

# Chapter Twenty-Two
## Phone Tag

It was Thursday, one week after the accident, and Lela was still too ashamed to show her face to Jake. She and Andrew were sitting in her living room staring at each other. When Lela had finally checked her messages on the evening of the accident, the voice of the police officer had brought her to her knees. Her instinct had been to send Andrew back to New York, but instead she had asked him to stay in town a few days longer. He obliged, moving into a local bed and breakfast.

It was in the breakfast nook, where they sat and talked about the past week. Andrew was a good listener... too good.

"Do you love him?" Andrew broke the silence.

"I don't know."

"Yeah, you do." He sat up straight in his chair. "Why don't you call him?"

"And tell him, what? Sorry I didn't come while you were in the hospital. I was too busy making out with my assistant."

"Okay. Tell him that."

"I'm serious."

"So am I."

"Why would I say that to him? It would just hurt him."

"And that's what you wanted all along, right?"

"What?"

"You wanted him to hurt, because he hurt you."

"That was years ago."

"Yeah, but you never got over it." Andrew leaned in. "You blame him for your rape."

"I do not!" She was infuriated.

"Yeah, you do." Andrew stated this matter-of-factly. "He dumped you to be a playboy and you fell right into the arms of someone you had no business being with. If he had kept his promise and married you, you wouldn't have gone to school so far away, and you wouldn't have dated Mr. Wrong. None of the events that followed would have happened. Is that how it plays out in your head?"

"No." She felt tears streaming down her face. "I would not do that. I'm not that type of person."

"Are you sure you're not?" Andrew stood and grabbed his bags and headed out the door. "I think you got what you were looking for."

"What's that?" She said as she watched him leave.

"Revenge." And with that Andrew was gone.

Lela wiped the tears from her face, knowing she wouldn't intentionally hurt Jake. She didn't need revenge. Did she? She picked up her phone and dialed the hospital but Jake had been checked out and was at home. She couldn't call him at home.

Another week passed and then another. Jake kept calling, Tristan called, too.

Lela stayed in her home and didn't answer the phone. Over and over she would listen to her voicemail and with every message Jake left, the hope in his voice faded as Andrew's words raged in her head: *You got what you were looking for.*

Finally, sick of the endless ringing, Lela answered her phone expecting Jake to be on the other end, but it was Tristan.

"Where in the hell have you been?"

"Busy."

"Busy with that boy toy of yours? Don't think Ms. Sutter hasn't given everyone a run down on you."

"You know what? I don't care about that nosy busy body!"

"Well, don't yell at me," Tristan clamored. "I hope you are dressed because I am coming over. I should be there in an hour."

"Tristan, no. I don't feel like company."

"I'm coming anyway. And I want the truth when I get

there."

# Chapter Twenty-Three
## Dangerous Encounters

Lela heard the door bell ring and expecting Tristan at any moment, she opened the door without asking who it was. It was a mistake she would never do again as she knew she was in trouble immediately and soon horror was all over her face. *I can't move,* she thought, *Oh God no... no.* Her eyes grew wide with panic, she tried to scream but her mouth wouldn't open. The man whose eyes were glaring at her snickered wickedly.

"I told you I would find you," Michael jeered.

Lela stepped back and with great force pushed the door toward him, but he caught if before it could close and forced it back, causing Lela to fall. She found herself in a frightening but familiar position. Vulnerable, she looked up to find Michael hovering over her with a deadly look on his face.

"You should have known better, Lela." Michael motioned toward his coat pocket. A cylinder shaped object protruded out of it. Lela scooted away from him, not letting her eyes leave his.

"You thought you could move out here in the middle of nowhere and hide from me."

"How?" She stammered, tears streaming down her face.

"Are you kidding? All I had to do was call your publisher. It's your own fault. Just like the last time."

"You bastard." Lela tried to stand but he stood over her and dared her to move. His movement dictated hers. Fear rang out in her limbs and she felt her body refuse to move further. "Please..." she begged, "please, go."

"Oh, I'll go." he taunted. "After."

Lela's eyes blurred over with tears. She could feel him lean down toward her. He gripped his fingers around her arm.

"You owe me," he hissed.

Lela kept her head down and tried to think about what she could do. *Scream*, she thought, but who would hear her? *Call 911.* Her thoughts raced. The phone was too far from where she was. Her eyes moved rapidly across the room, spotting all the heavy objects and books. *Fight*, she thought. *Fight.* She would not let him do this again. She would not let him take her power.

"Let's go." He grabbed her and forced her into her living room, throwing her on her couch. She kicked her legs up, hit his chin and threw him off balance. Lela saw an opportunity, jumped off the couch and reached for the nearest lamp, breaking it across his head.

"Ah!" he cupped his head with his hand. The impact only heightened his anger as he rushed toward her. Frantic, she shoved the coffee table in his path, shattering the glass, and then reached for anything she could fit in her hands and threw it at him -- books, pens, paper, her laptop.

"Leave me alone!" She yelled. "Go away!"

"I'll leave you alone... alright." Michael charged toward Lela and cornered her near her book case. Lela grabbed the bronze statuette that Jake had given her and rammed it against Michael's head. The impact was immediate, and he fell to his knees. She considered hitting him again, but saw that blood was already streaming from his head. Michael held his wound, and collapsed on the floor. Lela kept the statue in her hand as she stepped by him quickly. Her hands were trembling as she ran to her phone and dialed 911, keeping her eyes on him while she talked to the operator. She could see him try to get up but his injury was too severe.

# Chapter Twenty-Four
## Let it Go

Minutes seemed like hours to Jake as he rushed to Lela's house, his side still burning from his own injuries. Jake bumped into an officer as he passed through the door. The policeman was a member of Jake's church, and the person who had called Jake to tell him about Lela's situation.

"Thanks for letting me know." Jake nodded at the officer.

"It's no problem, man. She did a number on him though. She's a fighter."

"Yeah, she is."

"You should be at home though, getting some rest."

"No, I'm where I need to be."

Jake hurried toward Lela, who was now seated between two other officers, tissues in her hand. He watched as tears streamed from her eyes and soaked her tissue. She gave the officers her statement; her eyes were bloodshot and puffy. Jake looked over his shoulder to watch the paramedics as they placed a handcuffed Michael unto a gurney. His head was wrapped in a bandage. Lela took a deep breath as Michael was taken from the house, but she was obviously still very shaken.

"Don't worry ma'am," an officer said. "He won't be allowed to get out again. I promise you."

After the police left, Lela stayed on the couch and watched as Jake closed the door behind the officers. Quietness filled her home. She could hear the faint echo of the crickets outside. Jake sat beside her and wrapped his arms around her. She immediately pushed him away.

"Why are you here?" she asked.

"Because I care."

"I didn't come to your side. Why would you come to mine?"

"Because I care," he repeated.

"Stop it! Stop saying that!"

"But it's true," he said quietly.

"I didn't ask you to come."

"Sooner or later, Lela, you have to let go."

"Let go of what?"

"Of this anger you have toward me," Jake insisted.

Lela looked up at him. His eyes were stern but gentle.

"You don't think I know, but I do." He watched her closely.

"Why won't you let it go?" Lela hung her head. "You're not the one for me and I'm not the one for you. We are toxic." Her voice was just above a whisper and the words were hitting Jake like bullets shattering glass.

"Don't try and cut me loose, Lela. It won't work."

"Leave."

"Lela."

"Now."

"No." He stood firm. "I have loved you for as long as I can remember. Who else is going to love you like me?" Though he asked a question, he was afraid to hear an answer. He had heard about Andrew from Tristan and he wanted to know the truth.

"Why are you asking me this?"

"Tell me." Jake moved close again. "Does he love you?"

"Who are you talking about?" Lela turned away.

"Don't act like it never happened, Lela. Don't make me look like I'm crazy. Who is he?"

"No one."

"Look at me when you lie to me, Lela."

His pleading tone, took her by surprise. Jake didn't plead. She turned to face him and watched as tears flowed down his face.

"His name is Andrew and nothing happened."

"That's not what Tristan said."

"Oh, Tristan … what the hell does she know? She listens to Ms. Sutter." Lela stretched her arms.

"Did you sleep with him?"

"No." Jake searched her eyes for the lie but found she was telling the truth. "Don't get me wrong, I thought about it. And I played with the idea but I couldn't bring myself to share my body with a stranger."

"But you kissed him."

"Yes."

"And you did other things?"

"It doesn't matter now. What did or did not happen. Because he is gone and the point is, *we* are not meant to be."

"I don't believe that." Jake shook his head. "Why?"

"When you look at me, you don't see me, not the real me. All you see is a fairy tale. Two people reunited and love rekindled. It's not real. And I am not living in the world of make believe. I can't go the church banquets and couples' dinners. You would expect me to prance around and be this nice, cozy preacher's wife. I am a real woman with a lot of baggage and flaws … you don't want to acknowledge that."

"Fine, you have flaws. Who cares if you don't want to go to church dinners? I'll go by myself. I've never forced you to do anything you don't want to do."

"Yes, you do." She choked. "You silently impose these guilt trips on me. You never asked me if I wanted to be a part of that life."

"You already are."

"No, no, you assumed I was because I wrote a few books and sit in church on Sunday mornings, but that is not the same thing. I see the pressure you have on you, the responsibility to your congregation, to yourself."

"Lela, you have me confused. I don't know what you want. But I do know that I will never choose you over God. This is my calling and as much as I love you…" His voice trailed, then he noticed that she was shivering and the events that had taken place earlier that lead him there came back to his mind.

"I'm sorry. Now, is not the time." He pulled her back into his arms and held her close, not as a man who loves a woman but as a friend who loves a friend. Lela's body became limp and she leaned into Jake, her head fell into his shoulder and fresh tears began to flow. He held Lela like a father would hold a child who had just had a nightmare in the middle of the night, cradling her in his arms. The more she cried, the tighter he held her. He didn't speak a word for he didn't know what to say. So, he held her as securely as he could as a friend.

# Chapter Twenty-Five
## Silent Battles

Tristan's mother, Patience, sat quietly on the examining table and waited for her doctor to see her. Nervous with anticipation, she looked down at her hands and inspected her nails. *I should make an appointment at the salon*, she thought. Patience never missed a beat with her appearance; her hair was kept immaculate and her style could not be beaten.

Doctor Jones entered the examining room with Patience's health record in hand. She was tall, gangly but graceful and of middle age which did not show in her face. Doctor Jones made immediate eye contact with Patience. She pushed her long dark brown hair behind her ear and with the pen she held in her hand tapped the health record in front of her.

"I'm not going to sugar coat it Patience." She breathed in heavily-- as if the weight of the world was on her shoulders. "You have cancer."

"Cancer?"

"Breast cancer to be exact."

Patience clasped her hands together in emotional exhaustion. "What? How?"

"I know it is a bit of a shock, and you probably need time to digest this news and tell your family."

"Family?" Patience shook her head, "No... No... I will not be telling them. I don't want to worry them."

"If you wish." The doctor didn't flinch; as if she had heard those words before. "But you should seriously consider having a circle of support, maybe friends you can trust in." She continued. "Now, we have to start treatment immediately and aggressively."

"When?"

"Next week would be best." She opened the file to take some notes. "I have a specialist coming in on Monday and I would like you to see him. He is very good."

"Is he?" Patience was still reeling from the news.

"Yes." The doctor pulled out some literature from the file. "Also, I have referred your name to a support counselor here at the hospital, and you should expect a call before the end of the day."

"The day?"

"Yes, and here is some more information about local groups that you should take serious advantage of, especially if you don't plan on telling your family." She handed the pamphlets to Patience

"Family?" Patience murmured. She was neither here nor there and Doctor Jones recognized this.

"Patience," She placed her hand on her shoulder. "It's going to be okay. I am here to help you get well. We are all here to help you get well and you will." She said affirmatively, "You have to believe it though."

Patience looked her doctor in the eye. "I'll try."

# Chapter Twenty-Six
## Confessions

*You're nothing. You'll never amount to anything.*

Jeff could hear his mother's voice getting louder. He closed his eyes tightly and tried to ignore her banter, but it kept nagging him. *Your father was no good and you're just like him.*

He sat at the bar and gulped his third drink, in an attempt to drown out the noise in his head. Jeff had left work early, without telling his boss and without regret -- as if drawn to the local pit.. He had entered the bar and quickly started on rounds of dark liquor. What began as an occasional trip turned into an everyday stop before coming home. He tried to assure Tristan that it wasn't a big deal and that he could handle it but he knew he couldn't. Soon he started to skip work all together. He initially tried to avoid people he thought would spread the information back to his wife, but soon found that people who drink together usually stick together. His behavior, however, didn't go unnoticed. Jeff was a man who loved his appearance but Tristan and many others now observed his growing lack of care about his presentation, his breath constantly reeked of alcohol and mints. Tristan, though upset by his developing habits, felt she had to focus on her health and career. She was a little over four months pregnant and didn't want to stress herself out; so she evaded the issue and more than that she avoided her husband all together. Ever since she read Tanya's email she didn't know what the truth was and what a lie was. Now, she was too afraid to confront Jeff.

Jeff sat idle, gazing ahead of him into space.

"May I join you?" A woman came up from behind him, and

tapped him on his shoulder.

"Thanks, but no thanks. My wife might take objection."

"I don't see her. What kind of wife would leave a handsome man like you alone." Although nearly drunk, Jeff didn't want to find himself in any more trouble than he had already created, so he refused.

"Look, I said I'm not interested."

The woman eventually gave up and walked away. Jeff ordered another drink and gulped it down quickly. His cell phone rang so he reached into his trouser pocket to answer, and paused when he recognized the number from Capital Memorial Hospital, where Tanya worked. A wave of nausea swept over him. He was uncertain if he should answer, not knowing who was on the other end of the line but the phone's insistency begged him to answer.

"Hello."

"Is this Jeff Williams?" A male voice asked.

"Yeah, who is this?"

"Sir, I'm calling from the Capital Memorial Hospital."

"Yeah."

"I'm sorry to inform you, but your wife has had an accident."

"What?" Jeff's heart began to race. "There must be some mistake, my wife's name is Tristan Williams and she should be at work."

"Oh... I'm sorry, the name we have here is Tanya Spencer. She's not your wife?"

Jeff was confused by the mix-up, and then he remembered that Tanya had named him as her emergency contact at work a long time ago.

"No, but I know her, how is she?"

"You would have to be family for me to divulge that information."

"Hey, you called me and she put me down as her emergency contact, what more do you want?

"Sir, I'm sorry."

"Okay fine. I'm on my way."

Jeff entered the hospital lobby with remnants of alcohol still on his breath. He briefly considered calling Eugene and Tristan, but knew he would have to explain his presence so he decided against it. The hospital was sterile, with white and blue walls and filled with the scent of cleaning products and illness. Jeff walked quietly and located the reception desk. He shivered as he walked under an air vent and a gust cold air pushed through. Jeff was able to get the attention of the nearest nurse. Still buzzed from the alcohol, he demanded to see Tanya. Lucky for him, the man he had spoken to earlier had not informed anyone that he was not Tanya's husband, so he was directed to her room.

Jeff stepped into her room with caution, unsure of who else was in there. He saw that Tanya was awake, but in a slight daze. She looked over, not expecting to see him, his frame filled the door way.

"You have no right to be here!" she screamed, her tears were uncontrollable. "No right!"

"Hey, it's not my fault you didn't take my name off your next of kin information. Besides, I just wanted to be here for you." He walked toward her. "Both of you," he added, motioning toward her stomach.

"Leave! I don't need you."

"How is the baby?"

"Like you care." All she could think about was how she desperately wanted him to change his mind about her but he never did. "I want you to leave." She could barely breathe. "You should be used to it."

He ignored her plea. He had to know the truth.

"How's the baby?"

"There is no baby, Jeff. No thanks to you."

"You lost it?"

"You're so stupid, Jeff."

"What are you talking about?"

"You knew this baby was yours and you never called or said a word. But you'll run away and marry Tristan, when she lied about having your child."

"My wife is pregnant."

"Now, but she wasn't then. Any idiot could see that."

"You're lying."

"Oh, please... why should I care enough to lie to you? You're a drunk. You come in here liquored up, smelling horrible, acting like I'm supposed to be grateful for your presence. I don't want you here, Jeff." She cut her eyes at him. "Now get out."

Tanya wanted him to feel her pain, at any cost. The security guard had been notified of the noise and entered the room. Jeff knew better than to cause more of a scene so he left.

*Tanya was lying, right?* He asked himself. *Tristan wouldn't lie to me about a baby. Would she?* Jeff thought about how Tristan had never cried about the loss, how he never saw her show any signs of emotion. He had thought it was her way of coping. Tristan buried herself in work and stayed away from home, just as he buried himself in alcohol. He thought about her small shape. In the four months she was supposed to be pregnant she had never gained a pound. *But that's not unusual, is it?* He didn't know. He had never been invited to attend a doctor's appointment even though he asked about them.

Jeff's eyes began to flash with anger, but as quickly as it came, it left, as sorrow stepped in. He was weighed down by the news that his wife had trapped him into a marriage. Not able to comprehend what he had just heard, he suddenly felt real thirsty, his mouth began to water and his hands shook. He drove straight to the bar.

# Chapter Twenty-Seven
## Man of the House

Jake spent the evening at Lela's home. He watched her move through her house slowly, as she tried to get back into some type of routine but ultimately she would end up staring into space like she was stuck in time. It was then that Jake would redirect her and lead her to her couch or make her eat something. He removed the broken coffee table and all the glass that had earlier lain across her living room floor. He ran interference when people began to call. First her parents, who found out through family friends who worked for the police department.

"I realize that she is upset, but I need to talk to her," Georgia said with worry.

"I know Ma'am. I'm not trying to keep her from you. She's just not ready yet."

"I'll come over there, Jake!"

"I know you will and I know that you're worried, but she just doesn't want company."

"But you're there!"

"Ms. Georgia, this is not the time to be pulling rank. We have to do what's best for her and right now, what is best for her, is no company. I promise you, she will call you when she is ready to tell you what happened."

"Fine. But if anything else happens to her, I will hold you responsible, Jake!"

"I completely understand, but as long as I am here, nothing else will happen," he said assuredly.

Jake also ran interference with the local news reporters who got the story from the police and showed up unannounced. Jake quickly and aggressively showed them the preverbal door. Once that episode was over, Tristan called.

"What happened? I am sitting in my office and Madison comes in and informs me that by best friend was attacked! What the hell is going on?"

"Look, Tristan… I have this under control."

"Under control, oh no! I'm coming over there right now. I will hire a guard… what does she need?"

"Look, Tristan. I understand that you feel the need to be here for Lela, but what she needs is space, right now and more importantly, it is what she wants. So, you stay at work and do what you do and let me do what I do."

"Well, okay…" She paused. "Since you seem to have it under control. I should have called to let her know I wasn't coming. I just got held up here. This is my fault, isn't it"

"Tristan, this isn't about you." Jake hung up the phone.

Later that night, Jake held Lela until she fell asleep, then carried her to her bedroom and placed her under the covers. He watched her for a while as she slept, then spent the rest of the night working on her security system. Around one in the morning, he finally crashed on Lela's couch.

# Chapter Twenty-Eight
## A Bad Hangover

Friday afternoon was Tristan's standing salon appointment. Evelyn put the finishing touches on Tristan's hair then placed some extra curls in the front. Tristan admired her style in the mirror, then noticed out of the corner of her eyes that someone was watching her. It was Mrs. Wilken.

"Well hello, dear." Mrs. Wilken greeted. "How are you?"

"I'm doing ok."

"Yes, dear. I'm sure you are. How is Jeff? We've missed him at the shop."

"You've missed him?" Tristan was thrown.

"Well, he has been leaving work early a lot, according to my husband, and sometimes he doesn't come at all. Is he ill?"

Tristan was confused. She didn't know Jeff had been skipping work and knew Mrs. Wilken's words were more for fact finding than sincerity.

"Yes, he's ill. He has been trying to get over the flu," she lied.

"Oh, I hope he gets better. What about your brother, Eugene ... and Tanya ... are they alright?"

"Why wouldn't they be?"

"Ms. Sutter called me yesterday and told me she saw them coming out of the hospital."

"Well, Tanya is pregnant, so they were probably going for a check-up."

"Just as long as everyone is alright."

"Thank you for your concern."

Several hours later, Tristan looked at the clock from her bed, the red letters beamed three am and Jeff was not home. *He has never been out this late*; she thought and hoped that nothing was wrong. After speaking with Mrs. Wilken at the hair salon Mr. Wilken called her and told her he would have to fire Jeff if he could not be at work the next morning, sick or not.

Tristan got up from her bed and walked into her office where she kept her cell phone, she checked to see if he left any messages and he had not. Tristan paced in her hallway nervously until she heard the sound of keys rustling at the door. She waited for it to open. As it did, she watched as Jeff's hands slipped from the knob and he fell into entrance, causing the door to slam open and a painting that hung on the wall to crash to the floor, breaking its frame and cracking the glass.

"Stupid picture," Jeff babbled.

Tristan stood silently and watched as Jeff blundered into their residence. He closed the door, slammed it shut then kicked its base which caused the wall to rumble. The glass crunched beneath his shoes as he fumbled with the painting; he picked it up, only to drop it again. He finally gave up and left the mess on the floor. Jeff turned to walk toward his bedroom and saw Tristan watching him.

"Jeez Tristan, are you trying to scare me to death? Why didn't you say something?"

"Why didn't you come home on time?"

"On time, on time... Are you my babysitter now? I'm a grown man, I come in when I want and I go where I want."

"Like the bar! You're drinking way too much."

"You are not my mother."

"Thank goodness for that."

"Don't play that role, Tristan. You are not a victim here."

"I never said I was. I just want you to come home on time, call if you're going to be late, go to work and stay there all day."

"What I do is my business."

"No Jeff, what you do is our business. We are married, so you don't just ruin your life when you make these types of decisions. What you do affects both of us."

"So now, I've ruined your life." He paused, "Ha, that's rich. You trap me into marrying you and I ruined your life."

"Trapped?" Tristan face fell.

"Yeah, trapped. You knew I didn't want to get married, you knew it scared the hell out of me, but you just had to have your way. So you lied about being pregnant! I wonder if you're really pregnant now or are you faking again."

"I am not faking." She trembled.

"But you did lie to get me to propose to you, didn't you? Didn't you!"

"I thought I was going to lose you," she stammered.

"You didn't even give me a chance to choose you. You forced me into this marriage."

"We were together for nine years, Jeff. You could have said no at any time. Don't blame me for your choice."

"Who else is there to blame, huh?"

"Blame Tanya. Blame yourself."

"Don't start."

"You've been cheating on me for years! Everyone else knew it but me, so how is that Jeff? How stupid could I be?"

"Pretty stupid, Tristan, and since we are dishing all the dirt today, you might as well know that the baby she was carrying was mine."

Tears ran down her face in streams.

"I know, you bastard. She told me … but unlike you, I thought about how much I loved you and instead of calling you on it, I decided to let it go."

"You mean you decided to act like you were in control of something you weren't."

"I am in control."

"That's right, Tristan, play that game…" He rolled his eyes. "Stay calm, and don't get all flustered. You're the adult here and nothing will go down unless you approve it, right?"

"That's right." She stood up straight to look him in the eye. "So let's get this straight … you made the choice to marry me, I forced you into nothing. If you want to leave, then leave, but don't stand here and blame me for your failure as a man."

"Failure, so now I'm not a man?"

"Would a real man go drinking every night when he has a pregnant wife at home?   Would a real man cheat on his girlfriend when he's supposed to be in a committed relationship?"  Angry, she tried to control herself but it was time to say what she felt.  "You said you'd love me forever."

"Love you?" Jeff huffed, "I don't even know if I like you."

"You're drunk.  Go to bed."

"Don't tell me what to do."

"You're saying things you don't mean."

"How would you know what I mean?  You don't know me. When have you ever taken the time to talk to me?  You're so busy working that you don't even know I exist."

"How can you say that to me?"

"Just as easily as you can lie to me."  Jeff staggered passed Tristan and went into the living room and plopped on the couch.  His head was swimming and he could no longer stand erect.  Tristan left him there and went back to their bedroom. She collapsed on the bed in tears.

# Chapter Twenty-Nine
## Leave the Past Behind

"I don't need a sermon, Jake." It was Saturday morning, and Jeff was under the hood of Lela's car, changing the spark plugs. Tristan had called Jake that morning, emotionally wrecked. She spilled her guts about the previous evening, and then begged him to talk to Jeff. Jake, not wanting to leave Lela alone, asked Tristan to sit with her until he returned and he took her car to the shop. He was skeptical that Jeff would be there, but it seemed that the idea of possibly losing his job hit home, so he'd showed up the next morning.

The shop had been in the neighborhood for over 40 years and had a few spots of graffiti on its parameter, some of which had been repeatedly painted over. The inside was plain white with rows of shelves holding oil and car parts. The floor was hard cement. Every sound echoed loudly inside, even though the garage doors were closed.

"I never said you needed a sermon. I'm not here to preach to you, I just thought you might want someone to talk to."

"Bull! Tristan called you and told you I was a drunk and a cheat and I needed to be fixed. Let me tell you something, she made me what I am."

Mr. Wilken came out of his office and motioned for them to keep their voices down. There were a few customers that lingered around inside the waiting room and outside while monitoring their cars.

"She didn't make you drink, and she surely didn't make you cheat. You were good at that way before you married her."

"So you're judging me now." Jeff smirked.

"No. I'm just trying to make you look in the mirror at your actions. They do hurt other people."

"Did she tell you she trapped me? I bet she didn't even mention she lied about the baby."

"She told me, Jeff, and I'm very sorry. She had no right to do that." Jake moved so that he could get a better view of Jeff. "But two wrongs don't make a right."

"She lied to me."

"And you lied to her. No one is better than the other here."

"All these months I was thinking it was my fault she lost the baby, because I couldn't keep a job and she was working so hard. It turns out she was never even pregnant! Do you know how it feels to be lied to like that?"

"No."

"Exactly … but you're here trying to tell me I need to work things out. I don't think so."

"I've never experienced what you are going through. But I do know what it feels like to lose yourself in drinking and in women. Everything you are doing has almost nothing to do with Tristan and everything to do with how you feel about yourself as a man."

"So you got saved and it all became clearer to you, Jeff said with sarcasm.

"No, it took hard work, counseling and sobering up before it became clear to me. My salvation saved my soul."

"Well whoop-de-do for you. But I'm sick of this. I told her I was moving out today, anyway."

"Don't do that, don't leave her, man. She loves you, she knows what she did was wrong and wants to start over."

"Start over." Jeff put the hood of the car down and looked Jake in the eye. "How could we even begin to start over? We've done so much to each other. I've done so much."

"She's having your child."

"I'll take care of my child, don't you worry about that. I'm not my father."

"Oh, so now we get to it."

"Get to what?"

"The real person you're mad at."

"My father was so high and mighty, the revered preacher who abused his wife and son, and you think I am going to listen to you."

"Your father was a troubled man, but I am not him." Jake paused. "Jeff, you are not too far away from becoming everything you hated about him. You may not physically abuse Tristan, but mentally she is shattered. Do you think leaving is going to change your behavior or make you happier?

"I don't know."

"You say you don't care, but I hope that you listen to me. Don't make any decisions right now. You don't have the right perception, you're angry, you're hurt and rightfully so, but making a decision like leaving right now is something you can't take back Jeff. You can't take leaving back."

"Your car is ready, man." Jeff turned and walked toward the office, but he hesitated at the door. "I'll think about what you said."

"Before I go, Jeff, I will be preaching every Friday for the next few weeks..." Jake watched Jeff's body language to see if he should continue. "I would like you to come at least once."

"Yeah, maybe." He paused, "How's Lela?"

"She's alright. Doing better."

"So, you're really going to make a go with her, huh?"

"Make a go... no." Jake rubbed the back of his neck, "No, I am going to make her my wife one day, man. I am going to dedicate my life to serving her needs, and her wants. I am going to be that man she's always wanted."

Jeff looked at Jake with what seemed like a bit of admiration.

"Do you really think you can pull it off?"

"I know I can. It may take time but I know I will."

Even though she was still weary from her own ordeal, Lela pulled her chair over next to Tristan and tried to comfort her. "It's not over, you can survive this," she whispered, trying to keep their conversation from being heard by other patrons.

They sat in a coffee shop on the main stretch of road that turned into a major highway.  The aroma of coffee grinds, lattes, cappuccinos, and pound cake filled the shop.  The two women were seated in the far corner of the shop at a small wooden table.  Tristan had convinced Lela that it was time to get back out into society and even managed to get her to come out for coffee-- an event that quickly turned into Tristan spilling her guts about Jeff.

"Are you kidding?  My marriage is based on lies and my whole relationship is based on self-interest."

"You can change that."

"Not if he doesn't want to.  He's leaving me."

"I know you're afraid but he won't walk out on you."

"What if he does?" she stressed.

"This may seem harsh, but if he leaves, that is his choice. You can't force or trick a man to stay where he doesn't want to be."

"I knew it was wrong and I did it anyway..." she cried. "He'll never forgive me."

"I think he will.  You two just need time to figure it out."

"Time!  Time.  How much time do you think it will take?"

"I don't know, Tristan.  But if you two are going to seriously work things out, it will take time.  This is not an overnight forgive and forget type of thing, as you both have done some serious damage to your relationship.  But I know where you can start."

"Where?"

"With prayer."

"Pray."  Tristan huffed.  "That's your solution, prayer." Tristan was sick of it.  "It hasn't been working, God's not listening."

"He is always listening," Lela said firmly.

"Oh really?"

"Do you curse?"

"What?"  She was confused by the question.

"Do you curse?"

"It depends on who's listening."

"Why?"

"Because, if I feel like my mother wouldn't approve, I don't do it." Tristan smirked.

"Well, if your actions can be affected by your mom and she is not in the room to hear you, why can't God hear your prayers?"

Tristan looked down at her coffee and half eaten butternut bread; Lela always had a way of making things plain.

"It's not like I don't pray. I just get so frustrated."

"You were trying to hold on to a lie, so was he... How can you expect to hear God, when you and he decided that your lies were going to keep your marriage together? That protecting your lie was more important than the truth. Now that the truth is out, the real healing can begin. You two can start to get to know the ugly side of each other."

"Can it get worse?"

"Yeah, I expect it will, but you have to decide now, if you mean those vows you took."

"Pray, huh." She spoke softly. "I guess it's worth a try again." Tristan's eyes were sparkling from the tears. "I just want the pain to go away."

"I can't promise you anything, I have my own issues... but when I get real low, I remember that God loves me no matter what I have done --past or present. "

"You forget that?" Tristan thought Lela never faltered in her faith.

"Sometimes I forget and sometimes, honestly, I choose to ignore it." Hearing the words come from her own mouth made Lela's heart ache.

"Wow," was the only response Tristan could muster.

"But in spite of it all, I think that if Jeff never forgives you, you should forgive him anyway. God will be with you but you must take the first step."

The two were silent for a while, listening to the sounds of the shop. Neither knew what to say next. They didn't know how to express their pain without succumbing to it. Soon, Tristan grew weary of the coffee shop chatter and spoke.

"I have prayed until I was blue in the face, until tears have soaked my blouse and stained my pillows at night and heard nothing."

"I can't believe for you, Tristan. It's hard enough for me to hold on for myself."

"Yeah, it is hard..." Tristan sniffed. "I try, but it is so difficult when my world is falling apart all around me."

"Try again."

"How can you be so hopeful after what happened to you?"

"All I have is hope, and if I give that up... what will become of me? I mean, I'm alive. So.... I'm okay. So I chose to continue to hope."

Lela was drained from her conversation with Tristan but still managed to muster up some optimism from her experience. Her life had finally come to a turn and she believed it was going to get better but that it may take some time. For the first time in a long time, Lela was optimistic. There was freedom in the truth and it was coming out in droves.

Tristan left the coffee shop and not more than a half-hour later, Lela was hit by the writing bug. She called Jake to let him know that she would remain in the shop for a while, so that she could write freely.

*Try again gal, try again. Though the rain falls like a fist in anger, though silence pierces your ears, wild eyes seeking peaceful faces, lost minds seeking wisdom beyond the hallways of academia. Whose path do we follow... besides our own. There is no such thing as a follower, each makes their own decision, treads their own water, dreams their own dreams, whether good or bad. So try again gal, try again.*

"Busy?" Lela's mother stood by her daughter's table, holding shopping bags.

"Never, for you."

"Almost never."

"Well, I had to take some time for myself."

"You've been through a lot lately."

"And where have you been?" Lela asked.

"Shopping of course. Thanks for calling me." She sat down.

"I had coffee with Tristan." Lela divulged.

"How is she?"

"Emotionally, she's a wreck but physically, she seems fine."

"Well, that's to be expected, and you, how are you doing?"

"Ma', I'm fine."

Georgia glanced at her daughter with inquisitive eyes. Her daughter was so private. She had missed at lot of her life but had never wanted to press. Their relationship was not a close one but she always wished it would be. She raised Lela to be independent, almost to a fault and wished at times they could be friends -- not just mother and daughter. She really wanted to know about the attack but didn't want to seem intrusive.

"So, how's the book coming?"

"Well, I'm glad you asked, because the direction my book is taking is more of a personal tone and I think I should fill you in before it goes to press."

Georgia's interest was piqued, so Lela pulled out of her tote bag a packet of papers with scribbles and writings and placed it in front of her mother. Georgia glanced at the title, *Saved for a Season*, then looked at her daughter.

"What does it mean?"

"It means, I've been through a lot and sometimes my faith got caught up in this world's stupidity and sometimes I let my faith go..." Lela swallow hard as she tried to hold back the tears, "Some seasons were better than others, but despite what I've been through I'm still a believer and I love the Lord. I guess ultimately, I refuse to only be *saved* when it is convenient."

Georgia suddenly realized that for the first time, she was being allowed into her daughter's life. Not wanting to let the moment pass she grabbed her daughter's hand and smiled.

"I know exactly what you mean."

"You do?"

"It's not easy but it is worth the work." Georgia looked at the stack of papers that lay before her, "So I'm I the first to see this?"

"You're the first to see it in a written form, but my editor was the first to know though."

"I'll take it." Georgia smiled.

Lela and Georgia soon parted from the coffee shop but not from each other. Georgia took the liberty of driving Lela home in order to extend their time together.

When Lela arrived home she found Jake waiting on her porch.

"Why didn't you go inside?" she asked.

Lela had given Jake a copy of her house keys in case of future emergencies.

"I didn't want to give you an excuse to take a long time."

"A long time for what?"

"Getting ready to go to the Pastor's house."

Lela had forgotten about their plans to have dinner with Jake's Pastor and his wife.

"Do we still have to go?" Lela winced as she remembered their unfinished conversation.

"We don't have to do anything you don't want to do." he said with sincerity

"Well, since you're being so nice about it, I'll go." she chuckled.

"There's hope for us yet." he said.

# Chapter Thirty
### Voices

Jeff left work late to try and make up for lost time. Not wanting to go straight home, he stopped by the bar for a few drinks, and after several hours of nursing his broken ego he went home to talk to Tristan. But no one was there. He deliberated on whether he should pack his things and leave or wait to talk to her. Instead, he sat in the living room in complete darkness. Jeff wiped the sweat from his forehead and pressed his hands against his jeans. His palms were moist and his mouth was parched. Although he had just left the bar he began to feel thirsty. Every noise or car he heard pass by his home made him leap to the window to see if it was Tristan. He paced his living room and became more frantic as time crept by.

*I should leave*, he thought, but he had nowhere to go. He couldn't leave her, no matter what happened --he loved her and always had. *She'll never forgive me*, he thought. *How can I forgive her?*

He could hear his mother's voice haunting him; *You're just like your father! You'll never be any good for a woman.*

"Shut up!" Jeff spoke out loud. "Shut up, it's not true."

Jeff's mother had caught him with another girl while he was dating Tristan and told him he was destined to follow in his father's footsteps.

"I'm not him!" Jeff hissed out-loud, "I'm not." *Sure you are,* his mother's voice returned, *you're just as bad. You should leave her before she leaves you. You're going to lose her. You are no good and you'll never be any good.*

"Stop it!" He needed the voice to stop. He knew that Tristan kept a bottle of champagne around for special occasions, so he ran into the kitchen and found the bottle. It took him less than five minutes to down it. It wasn't enough. He could still hear his mother's voice. He stumbled his way to the bathroom cabinet, where they kept their medications and downed a bottle of prescription pain killers. He just wanted the voice to go away.

Though nervous, Lela felt at home from the moment she stepped through the marble inlaid threshold of Pastor and Mrs. Mitchell's home. Mrs. Mitchell greeted Jake and Lela with a big broad smile and hugs. She led them into the living room where Mr. Mitchell waited. The home had high ceilings, was brightly lit and nicely warm and the aroma of pecan pie filled the air. The hallway to the dining room was lined with family photos of the Mitchell's three children as youth and adults with families of their own. The Pastor and his wife were in their late fifties and seemed to be classically styled partners, with time-tested values.

"We picked up a cake from you and your wife's favorite bakery on the way here." Jake displayed a beautifully adorned German chocolate cake to the couple.

"Wow, you two didn't have to go to any trouble," Mrs. Mitchell exclaimed as she took the cake and made her way to the kitchen. "But we will definitely cut into this one tonight!" she yelled from the kitchen, and then swiftly returned to the living room with a tray of appetizers. She invited everyone to try the delightfully arranged water crest sandwiches and mini sausages, to which Jake and Mr. Mitchell immediately obliged. Lela chose to follow Mrs. Mitchell's lead and let the men have at it.

"Would you like some help in the kitchen?" Lela offered.

"Well, you can help me carry out the dishes, but the meal is done." Mrs. Mitchell motioned for Lela to follow and they left the men to finish off the starters.

Once in the kitchen, Lela complimented Mrs. Mitchell on her decorating and admired her modern cork flooring. Mrs. Mitchell accepted the compliments graciously, and pointed Lela to the dishes they were going to use. As Lela handled the plates, Mrs. Mitchell watched her closely.

"You're used to being in the kitchen?"

"Yes, my mother taught me how to cook very early."

"That's good." She commented quietly. "So, how long have you and Jake known each other?"

Lela knew that was Mrs. Mitchell's way of asking, what are you two doing together?"

"Well, we have actually known each other since we were teenagers. We went to the same high school."

"Oh, really? Were you close then?" In other words, did you date?

"Yes." Lela one-worded.

"Mmmmm." She returned and waited for an additional response. Lela finally caved.

"It was serious for a while, and then we broke up when I was in college."

"Mmmmm." She countered, and again waited for more.

"We reunited at a mutual friend's wedding and we have been hanging out ever since."

"Hanging out?"

"Well, we're just friends. I mean, we talk. That's all. Just talk."

"Mmmmm."

Lela felt like she had told too much but it was too late to take it back now.

"So, how long have you and Pastor Mitchell been married?" Lela asked, deciding to turn the questioning around.

"Thirty years this December." Mrs. Mitchell said it with the same big broad smile she gave when she greeted them at the door.

"That's wonderful."

"Well, it was no easy road, but it was a road worth traveling." She picked up a large bowl filled with salad. "Let's go get the men."

Again, Lela followed Mrs. Mitchell's lead and picked up a bowl of asparagus and walked into the dining room, where they laid the food on an immaculately set antique dining table.

"Dinner!" called Mrs. Mitchell.

Jake and Pastor Mitchell filed into the room. Then as indicated by Pastor, the four joined hands for prayer.

"Precious Lord. Heavenly Father. Thank you for this young couple that joins us here tonight. I pray that you will watch over them and aid them in their decision making, now and into the future. Thank you for my wonderful wife and for all the hard work she has put into preparing this meal. Bless this food for the nourishment of our bodies. In Jesus name, I pray. Amen."

"Amen." The trio followed.

As Lela sat down, she wondered what Pastor Mitchell had meant about helping her and Jake make a decision. What decisions? She would have to remember to ask Jake after dinner.

Soon the conversation turned to marriage. It seemed to be the topic whenever Jake and Lela were around.

"It was not easy," Mrs. Mitchell said as they conversed over baked halibut, potatoes and asparagus. "We had our ups and we've definitely had our downs."

"But we held strong in the roughest time because we were both too stubborn to let the other one get off that easy." Mr. Mitchell joked.

"Stop it." Mrs. Mitchell laughed as Lela and Jake exchanged looks. "No, really it is a great marriage but not without its scares."

"So, you two seem comfy?" Mr. Mitchell said through a grin at Jake, making Lela choke on her fish. She began to cough lightly.

"Well, we're friends."

"Hah!" It would seem that the Pastor was less capable of the art of suggestion than his wife.

"I mean. We're good friends."

"Sure you are. Good friends always stay over at each other's home." Mrs. Mitchell said.

"Stay over, who stayed over to whom?" The Pastor sat back.

Jake rubbed his forehead in annoyance. "Look, there is nothing inappropriate going on between Lela and me, so I am going to leave it at that."

"Ms. Sutter doesn't think *nothing* is going on."    Mrs. Mitchell's words floated across the table on a wave of judgment that ended right at Lela's ears.

"Ms. Sutter is a gossipy witch, who has nothing to do with her time than to take things that could be completely innocent and turn them into the hottest tabloid incidents."   Lela was hot. "And anyone who takes anything she says seriously is an idiot."

"Lela," Jake cautioned.

"No.   Wrong is wrong, even for a Pastor's wife."   Lela looked Mrs. Mitchell in the eye.   "You want to know what's going on between us?"

"You don't have to do this," Jake interrupted.

"No. I need to."  Her eyes stayed on Mrs. Mitchell, whose face was flustered.    "Jake has been the most caring and supportive friend that I could have.  He has been there for me during a very difficult time in my life, and all the while asking for nothing in return."  Her eyes became puffy with tears and she gasped.  "Yes, Jake has spent the night at my house.   It's really none of your business why, but since your twisted ignorant mind would like to go to the nastiest explanation instead of reasonable ones, I am going to tell you why."

"Lela, don't."

"No really, she needs to hear this.  So she can go and run and tell Ms. Sutter and they can go tell the world.  I was attacked about a week ago, in my home, by a man who wanted to kill me. This same man raped me when I was in college."  Lela paused for a reaction but received none from the stunned Pastor and wife.  "You two are a little too silent.  What ... no questions? Well. Let me fill you in.  I don't feel safe in my home, so Jake has been staying with me, to alleviate my anguish."  She sighed heavily and sat back.  "So I hope you're happy.  Ms. Sutter knows nothing about my struggle, nothing, and neither do you."

"We apologize," Pastor Mitchell said.  "Don't we, Grace."

Mrs. Mitchell looked shell shocked and shamed into silence, so she nodded her head in embarrassment and submission. "So if you are willing to forgive us, we can all finish our meals and then Jake and I will cut into that cake."

Lela saw kindness in the Pastor's eyes and knew he was sincere. He couldn't help that fact that he had married a busy body, so Lela nodded her head in agreement and forgiveness.

"Quick to forgive, she is!" said Pastor. "That's good, and it will come in handy in the future."

Tristan entered her home after wandering around the town for hours. She was in no rush to get home and find Jeff gone and felt more strained than ever. She had made up her mind to talk to Jeff and ask him to attend couple's counseling with her. As she entered the door to her home, she knew immediately something was wrong. There was an empty champagne bottle in the middle of the hallway.

"Jeff." She yelled down the hallway, but he did not answer. Tristan made her way to their bedroom and found Jeff lying face down on the floor in a pool of vomit. Tristan panicked.

"Jeff!" she screamed kneeling down by his side. "Jeff wake up!" She shook him forcefully, with no results. Tears began to stream down her face as she spotted the empty pill container.

"Oh, Jeff..." she sobbed. Then she ran to the phone and called 911.

"911, what's your emergency."

"My husband."

"Ma'am calm down. Tell me what's going on."

"My husband... he's passed out." She moaned. "Oh God, I think he's dead."

# Chapter Thirty-One
## Forgiveness

After a few hours of hearing nothing Tristan began to be anxious. She fidgeted with her cell phone, checking to make sure it was still working, then called her mother and her sister. When she didn't get an answer, she left another message. Lela's cell phone kept going straight to voicemail and no one had called her back. She felt isolated and alone. She occasionally asked the nurse for an update, only to be given more papers to fill out. She sat in the waiting room listening to the sounds of people rushing in and out. She saw an elderly man come in on a gurney with paramedics on either side of him. His face was gray and blotchy and he was grasping for air. He was followed by a processional of people, including an elderly woman with salt and pepper hair who was being supported by a younger woman. Both had looks of concern and distress on their faces. *At least they have each other*, Tristan thought, then she felt her phone vibrate in her hand and checked its caller ID. When she saw Lela's number, she answered quickly.

"Come quickly. I'm at the hospital. Jeff tried to commit suicide," she said without taking a breath.

"I'm on my way." Lela hung up and looked over at Jake with urgent eyes. Without explanation he knew they needed to leave and they hastily bid their farewell to the Pastor and his wife to drive to the hospital.

Jake and Lela arrived and found Tristan seated in the lobby with Camille.

"What's going on?" Jake asked with concern as he glanced

from Camille to Tristan. "Are you alright?" he asked Tristan.

She looked stunned.

"We're fine." Camille squeezed Tristan's hand. "Jeff is ill."

"Well, what happened? How's he doing?" Lela asked.

"They haven't said." Tristan looked horrible, as if she had been through a fire storm. "What am I going to do if he dies?"

"Don't think like that." Lela wrapped her arms around Tristan. "He is going to be just fine."

"What happened?" Jake interjected.

"He tried to kill himself, that's what happened. What did you say to him this morning?" Tristan jabbed.

"What? I talked to him, like you asked me to. He was fine when I left him."

"Fine!" Tristan stood. "My husband is in a hospital being treated for an overdose. Does that sound like fine?"

"Tristan, you don't honestly think Jake caused this?" Camille questioned.

"What am I supposed to think? He has never considered suicide, ever! The one day Jake talks to him, he goes off on the deep end. Whose fault is it?"

"It's no one's fault," Lela replied. "Look, you're scared. We understand, but don't start throwing out accusations. Besides Jeff is going to be ok."

"Why? Because God is watching over him?" Tristan huffed, "While I was praying, my husband was lying on the floor dying. What kind of God does that?"

"I know it's hard to see right now, but God does love you and Jeff," Jake replied.

"He has a funny way of showing it. He was supposed to forgive me, not punish me."

"He is not punishing you," Camille said comfortingly.

"What do you call this?"

"I don't know, but I know that this is not God's doing. You have to stay strong," Camille reiterated.

"Since when do you talk about God? You don't even go to church!"

"Tristan. I know you're hurt, but Camille is right ... you

have to stay strong," Lela chimed in.

"I don't have to do anything!" Tristan looked Lela in the eyes. "Jeff was right, it's all for nothing."

"You don't believe that Tristan," Jake spoke. "You know you don't believe that it's nothing."

Jake could see Tristan's frustration and wanted to be there for her, but couldn't allow her to vent in such a negative way.

"When will it end, Jake, when will this be over?"

"When you let go of the control."

A short stubby man in a long white smock came out to see Tristan. He approached assertively, his shoes squeaking from overuse, his I.D. tag dangling from his chest pocket.

"Mrs. Williams." He looked over the rim of his glasses directly at Tristan.

"How's my husband?" she asked.

"He'll be fine. We were able to pump his stomach." Not breaking eye contact, he added, "We need to keep him over night for a psych evaluation."

"Why?"

"Ms. Williams, your husband drank excessive amounts of alcohol and downed a vast amount of pain killers. It is obvious that he has had some kind of mental break down."

"Break down."

"It's hard to hear, I know. But he may need some serious help."

"Can I see him? I need to see him."

The doctor nodded and escorted Tristan to Jeff's room, leaving Camille, Jake and Lela waiting in the lobby.

The room was dim. All the curtains were closed. Jeff lay facing the window, his back to the TV monitor in a corner that was silently displaying the news. As Jeff stared at the blank white walls, he heard Tristan approach from his back. Her walk was fast paced and her heels clicked heavily as if she always had somewhere imperative to go.

"You shouldn't be here," he said.

"Of course, I should. You're my husband." She could hear

the strain in his voice.

"I don't want you to see me this way."

"If I can't see you at your worst and still love you, what good am I as a wife?"

"An obedient one."

"This is not the time to be pulling that crap, Jeff. I'm not going anywhere."

Jeff inched is body over to face Tristan. His stomach and lower abdomen were sore and he felt like hot coals were being forced down his throat. Tristan made her way to her husband's side and sat on his bed. She brought her lips to his forehead.

"I don't care about what you did, I care about you. I forgive you and I ask that you forgive me." She nuzzled his ear. "Do you think you can do that?"

"I can try." Jeff cried, "But there is something else you need to know."

"Right now the only thing I need to know is that you are focused on getting better."

"Tristan... listen." Jeff paused. "I'm sorry. I was wrong to blame you and I was wrong for what I did, but I never meant to hurt you."

"It doesn't matter anymore."

"Listen!" He spoke through the pain. "I hated that you went away to school without me. I hated it when you decided to go to law school. I hated your career and I always thought that one day you would wake up and realize you didn't need me and that you would leave."

Tristan breathed in deeply and fought back her tears.

"I'm sorry I was not the man you needed me to be."

"You were all the man I wanted and needed. Like I said, we will handle that later. Right now you must get better."

"Really?" Jeff was surprised by her empathy.

"Yes. Despite what happened."

"Are you still willing to forgive me?"

Tristan grinned through her tears. "I have to Jeff. It's the only way I can make it right." She kissed him on the forehead again and pulled his blanket up to keep him warm. "I'll be here all night. I just want to send Cami, Jake and Lela home."

Jeff rested his head on his pillow and watched Tristan leave the room, assured that she would return. He thought about her words. *She loves me*, he thought.

Tristan went back to the lobby, where she was happy to see that the three of them were still there. She was glad that they had not abandoned her in spite of her comments earlier.

"I'm so sorry," she babbled.

"No need to be," Lela smiled. "How is he?"

"He'll be fine. I'm going to stay the night, but I'll call you guys tomorrow." She looked at the floor. "Thank you for coming."

"Wouldn't have it any other way," Jake replied.

Saved for a Season

# Chapter Thirty-Two
### Resisting Temptation

Jake and Lela rode home together. As the evening rolled on the night air became crisp. Jake came to a stop in front of Lela's home. He had been sleeping on her couch for the past week, since the attack-- but tonight he knew he needed to stay in his own apartment. He looked over at Lela and admired her beauty. She had her locs pulled up, just as she had the night of the wedding.

"So, I'm thinking that I'll come in and check the place out, make sure it is secure, then go home."

Lela knew he was right. He couldn't stay with her forever, or could he?

"How about you stay tonight, "she said. "It's late."

"You know that I can't be your crutch. You have to be able to move on. If you need someone to stay with you, call your parents. People will certainly begin to talk if I stay any longer."

"We're not twelve, Jake."

"Exactly, that's why we have to make responsible decisions. I'm a minister, Lela. I cannot continue stay here."

"So, Mrs. Mitchell's words got to you."

"No." Jake's face grew warm. "You get to me."

Jake's words weakened Lela, and she bit the inside of her cheek. A rush of sensation filled her body

"Lela, know that I love you and that I respect you, but I am still a man."

Lela felt her face grow warmer. "You don't have to explain."

"I think, I do." He turned to look at her. "I cannot stay in the same home with you, watch you walk around in your night gowns, even if they are covering everything. I can't continue to hold you until you fall asleep and…." His voice began to trail off.

"I hear you, Jake. You really don't have to explain any further."

"I know, but I want you to know that I am truly attracted to you and being so close to you, in this way is not good for me. Especially since we are supposed to be taking it slowly and especially because we can't do anything about it, unless you want to get married tonight."

"Hah," Lela laughed. "Married … wouldn't that be something."

"I know." He smiled.

"You're not alone in this, you know," Lela replied. "I just want you to know it's all a part of my ever conflicting emotions."

Jake smiled at the reference and Lela really felt that he understood where she was coming from.

"Okay, so come and check the place first, so I don't feel completely freaked out."

"Oh, now you're going to make me feel bad." Jake smiled.

The two went inside and Jake went about securing the home. Lela disappeared into her bedroom.

"Let me know when you're ready to go. I want to give you something." She yelled from her private quarters.

Twenty minutes later, Jake knocked on her bedroom door.

"Lela, I'm ready to go."

"Come in, first."

Jake entered to find Lela standing over her dresser with her anxiety pills in hand. She walked over to Jake and handed him the bottle.

"Do me a favor and get rid of these for me."

"I'm glad to see that you are ready to give them up."

"After what happened to Jeff, I could just see myself in the same position. All you want to do is take the pain away, not realizing that you're hurting yourself in the process."

Jake took the pills and walked straight into the bathroom and poured the whole bottle into the toilet. He motioned for Lela to join him and she did.

"You flush," he ordered. She followed his lead and flushed the pills.

"No more blue magic," she jokingly pouted.

"We'll make our own magic," he replied.

# Chapter Thirty-Three
### Line in the Sand

Tristan watched her husband as he slept. Throughout the night nurses and orderlies stopped by to take Jeff's blood pressure and check on his status. Despite the busy atmosphere of the emergency room, Jeff's room was quiet after the noise died down and the hallways became scarce with activity. The local hospital emergency room closed. Tristan took advantage of the moment and left Jeff asleep to wander around the halls. She rubbed her belly gently, circling her belly button. Her stomach was now protruding, though not much, but she noticed the change. She decided to visit the natal unit where a skeleton crew was feeding a few of the babies and rocking some to sleep. She gazed at their tiny bodies, their feet covered with booties and heads with cotton knit caps. *They're so innocent,* she thought.

Tired from the stressful day, she headed back to Jeff and called it a night, falling asleep on a cot placed in the room for her.

"Tristan." She was awakened by her brother, who was standing above her with two cups of coffee in his hands. She squinted her eyes, trying to block the bright lights that were bearing down on her.

"What are you doing here?"

"Tanya works here, remember? She found out about Jeff this morning and called me."

"Tanya."

"Yeah, why didn't you call me?"

"Because it wasn't necessary."

"You shouldn't be here alone. Not in your condition."

"I wasn't here alone, Lela was here last night, and she is going to come back today." Tristan sat up, stretching her back. "Anyway I'm pregnant not dying."

Eugene looked over to Jeff, who was still sleeping.

"How is he?"

"The doctor says he is going to be fine, physically, but needs to be evaluated before he can be released."

"Released." He paused. "Maybe you should come stay with me for a while, until things can be straightened out."

"What? I'm not leaving my husband."

"The man is unstable, Tristan." He whispered, "He could seriously hurt you."

"Stop." Tristan's face hardened. "Don't say another word about my husband or you and I will not be on good terms."

"I admire your loyalty, but you shouldn't be putting yourself in harm's way."

"I don't care what you admire, Eugene. This is not your marriage … it's mine. If you want to be supportive then give me that coffee and stop antagonizing me."

Eugene handed his sister the cup and stepped back to take a seat in a nearby chair. "So you know about Tanya."

"What about her?" Tristan was rubbing her neck.

"She lost the baby."

"Wow, well that explains even more about what Jeff was feeling."

"Jeff? What does he have to do with it?" Eugene gaffed.

"Don't play dumb, Eugene, it doesn't suit you."

Tristan stood, realizing that her brother had no idea what she was talking about and that Tanya must have lied in the email. She knew her brother would never betray her that way but she decided to take a cue from Lela's book. It was not her place to give details. Eugene watched her tighten up.

"Look, you don't have to stay. I'm fine and Jeff will be okay. So, you should go check on your fiancé."

"My fiancé is doing ok. I told you she's back at work."

"Well, then go home," Tristan said.

"You don't want me here?"

"No, Eugene, I'm sorry but this doesn't concern you." She walked to the door and opened it for him to leave. "I appreciate your concern, but really, I got this."

"Ok, I'll go," Eugene agreed. "I guess I shouldn't tell mom."

"Tell her or don't tell her, it doesn't matter anymore. I can't live my life determined by what you all think of me. I'm finished with that type of life. I'm going to start focusing on what's important."

"What's more important than your family?"

"Jeff is my family," she said firmly. "I've been living my life according to what you all say is right for too long." Tristan shook her head. "No more. I'm drawing the line."

# Chapter Thirty-Four

## Share a Testimony

Jake was knee deep in prayer and did not hear Lela walk up behind him. She watched as he prayed silently, barely moving his lips. He was kneeling before the prayer alter of his church, holding a piece of paper with some writing on it. His eyes were shut, which caused a lone crease to appear around his forehead and stretch to his hair line. Not wishing to interrupt his prayer, she sat on the front row closest to the pulpit, and watched him. His long legs were bent and his knees rested on the cloth covered cushioned bench and his body leaned against a low wooden rim. He occasionally rocked back and forth, and raised his voice -- only to quiet down after a few minutes of praise and talk in a whisper of prayer again. After a while, his lips stopped moving and he stopped rocking.

Jake opened his eyes and stretched his arms out wide. He stood, still facing the pulpit. Though not mouthing any words and no longer kneeling, Lela still felt he was praying, so she kept quiet.

"Are you ever going to announce yourself?" he asked.

"I thought you were still praying." She looked at his back, still not moving.

"That was nice of you. Most people would interrupt me anyway."

"I'm not most people."

"Do you want to join me?" He turned around to face her, seeing that she was seated, her arms placed gingerly on her lap and her legs crossed at the ankles. *She's a lady*, he thought.

"Join you in what?"

"Prayer, Lela."

"Oh…" She paused. "That's not why I came."

"I know, but if you have the time, I think we should pray for our friends." Jake was somber.

"I would be happy to," she answered. "And maybe we can pray for each other, too." She stood and walked over to his side, taking his hand in hers.

Several Fridays later, Jake's church was packed with people from all over the county. Although the air conditioner was running, the heat from the bodies made the sanctuary temperature rise and ushers were busy handing out fans. The historic hall was adorned with flowers and a dim light shone through the stained glass windows.

Jake, wearing jeans and a polo shirt, walked up to the pulpit. He placed his bible on the podium and bowed his head in silent prayer before motioning for the congregation to stand and join him in a hymn. When the organ ceased playing and the voices had died down from praise, Jake gave his acknowledgements and prepared to begin his sermon.

"Good Evening, Church!"

"Good Evening," the congregation responded.

"Today is a good day in the name of our Lord and Savior, Jesus Christ." Jake left the pulpit and stepped down to be on the same level as the congregation. "Before I get into the word today, I want to tell you my testimony." He looked in Lela's direction. She, Tristan and Jeff were seated in the front row.

"God saved me three times." He paused. "I had a great career, I was smooth with the ladies but I was lost. I went to bed, almost every night and would wake up every morning, feeling empty. I was lost …trying to find who I was through money, women, drinking …alienating myself from the people I truly cared about."

Jeff hung his head. He had never known what Jake had gone through.

"I told you earlier that God saved me three times, which I

can count. I am sure there were so many other times when he saved me from myself, but these three are what brought me before you this day. The first was when he saved me from HIV/AIDS and the second was when my brother in Christ, Kevin … led by God … found me when I tried to commit suicide. And the third was when I decided to accept Christ as my personal savior."

Jake made eye contact with the congregation. "I went to his church. It was there that I heard a man preach about how he had come to Christ. His story was not my story, but the pain was the same. I was looking for my purpose and it wasn't in women, or money, or drinking, it was in God. I found out that night, that God loved me, and that I was handpicked to be his child and that no matter where I came from or what I had done, He would love me and accept me. "Amen," members of the congregation responded.

"All I had to do was repent of my sins and accept Jesus as my personal savior. Friends, my soul was saved that day." Jake walked back up the steps to the pulpit, and opened his bible. "Friends the word for today comes from Romans 10:9-11; *that if you confess with your mouth, 'Jesus is Lord,' and believe in your heart that God raised him from the dead, you will be saved. For it is with your heart that you believe and are justified, and it's with your mouth that you confess and are saved. As the scripture says, 'anyone who trusts in him will never be put to shame."*

After the sermon, Lela waited for Jake. When he emerged from the side exit, she felt her heart leap. It was happening. She was truly falling for this man all over again, but he wasn't the same, he was a new man. A man she had to take the time to get to know. Jake had a wide smile on his face.

"So?" Lela baited him

"The pastor said I did a good job and asked me to lead the young adult ministry. He said they could learn from my mistakes."

"Congratulations."

"Yeah, I'm pretty happy with that."

"You spoke very well."

"Thank you. It was a good crowd today, and they were very receptive."

"Yeah, they were."

"Why didn't you stay inside? I wanted you to stand beside me as I shook everyone's hands, as the dutiful wife." Jake playfully poked her in the shoulder as Lela shook her head.

"I don't' think so."

"No." Jake's smile widened. "Oh, you don't know?"

"What?"

"That I've already claimed you." he chuckled.

"Excuse me? Claim. I am not airport baggage, Mr. Carson," she jeered.

"Oh, it's Mr. Carson now ... so formal."

"As long as I'm baggage, you'll be Mr. Carson," she teased.

"Okay, Okay. I give up. I guess I should be use to that." He smiled.

"You should be."

The two stared at each other for a while in silent amazement.

"I really didn't expect my life to end up like this, you know," Jake stated.

"Like what?"

"Happy with uncertainty."

Lela laughed. Jake looked like a kid in a candy store.

"So, what now?"

"You tell me?" he stated with a bit of mystery.

"What?" Lela chuckled.

She was unsure what Jake was talking about. Then she watched him as he pulled a small velvet box out of his coat pocket, holding it as if it were an egg in his hand. Jake watched as Lela's eye got wide, then knelt in front of her. Congregants who had not left the church grounds began to huddle closer to watch the two.

"Well, I was thinking about what you said, about us not being meant for each other. And I have decided that you're wrong," he said firmly. "Lela, I love you, and one day I think we should get married." He breathed. "I know we will"

"Oh, goodness, Jake." She paused and knelt, facing him. She didn't mind that the concrete was pushing into her knees. "Do you ever learn?"

Jake nodded in the affirmative then placed the box in her hands.

"Open it."

"We are not ready."

"Open the box, Lela," he commanded. Curious, she opened the box to find it empty. Confused she looked up at him. He smiled with cryptic eyes.

"What is this about?"

"Time," he said. "It's about time. I'm not going anywhere and this box is a reminder to you, that I'm not going anywhere." Then Jake opened his hand to reveal a deep blue sapphire stone surrounded by diamonds. "And this ring will stay in this box until you realize that it's time."

Lela met Jake's gaze and smiled.

"All I want is time," he said.

Saved for a Season

# Chapter Thirty-Five
## New Beginnings

"You have been a light in my darkness. Your forgiveness and enduring love is one that I will always treasure. I promise to honor and respect you, to treat you as my queen, virtuous and wise. I will be the man that God has called me to be and love you as 'Christ loves the church;' without reservation and without end. My love is longer than a river and deeper than an ocean."

Lela looked deep into Jake's eyes, holding her bundle of tulips at her waist. Jake was standing between Jeff and Tristan, who was prompting him to get the ring. Jake smiled over at Lela, who was witnessing the ceremony between Jeff and Tristan as they took their vows in the proper way. This time there were few guests -- just four friends, and they were dressed in simple attire, standing on the sandy shore of Bay Beach. The tide was slowly coming in, washing their feet in a gentle pass as the sun glimmered on the gulf waters, creating a glowing path that floated across the waves. A tear ran down Tristan's cheek as she smiled, overwhelmed by the moment.

"Do you take this man to be your lawfully wedded husband? For better or for worse, for richer or for poorer, in sickness and in health, to have and to hold, from this day forward, for as long as you both shall live?" Jake asked.

"I do," Tristan answered.

Jake then turned to Jeff. "Do you take this woman to be your lawfully wedded wife? For better or for worse, for richer or for poorer, in sickness and in health, to have and to hold, from this day forward, for as long as you both shall live?"

"I do," Jeff answered.

"Then by the power invested in me by God and the State of Florida, I pronounce you husband and wife. You may salute your bride." Jake smiled.

Lela smiled as the two kissed. She looked over at the sunset as it finished its decline over the ocean. She looked over at Jake and wondered if they could ever make it to this point. She hoped so.